Francis Henry Underwood

The Poet and the Man

Francis Henry Underwood

The Poet and the Man

ISBN/EAN: 9783743367463

Manufactured in Europe, USA, Canada, Australia, Japa

Cover: Foto ©Andreas Hilbeck / pixelio.de

Manufactured and distributed by brebook publishing software (www.brebook.com)

Francis Henry Underwood

The Poet and the Man

THE POET AND THE MAN

RECOLLECTIONS AND APPRECIATIONS

OF

JAMES RUSSELL LOWELL

.

BY

FRANCIS H. UNDERWOOD LL.D.

FORMERLY U. S. CONSUL AT GLASGOW
AUTHOR OF "QUABBIN" "HANDBOOKS OF ENGLISH LITERA-
TURE" "THE BUILDERS OF AMERICAN
LITERATURE" ETC.

BOSTON
LEE AND SHEPARD PUBLISHERS
10 MILK STREET
1893

THE POET AND THE MAN

TO

OLIVER WENDELL HOLMES

It seems not only appropriate but almost oblig-
atory to dedicate these Recollections to you, —·
Lowell's life-long friend, associated with all
memories of old Cambridge, and the last of an
historic group of authors whose fame is the
pride of New England.

i

PREFATORY

THIS Memoir is wholly distinct from the author's Biographical Sketch, which was published about a dozen years ago, while Lowell was Minister to Spain.

The author's intention is to furnish in compact form the important facts in the poet's life, with a brief account of his works, and to record some personal impressions and reminiscences. For several years the author lived in Cambridge, and was one of a circle of half a dozen of Lowell's friends which met frequently at Elmwood and elsewhere. His opportunities for knowing the poet in his brightest days were exceptional. As most of the members of that circle are dead, it seems to be something like a duty for the author to recall and fix his impressions before they become dim. No faithful study, made at first hand, of the character and personal traits of such a remarkable and richly endowed man, can be without interest and value.

Within the limits of a small volume like this, there can be few details or discussions: for any fulness of statement and for an adequate analysis of Lowell's works, the reader must wait until a biography on a larger scale shall appear. This Memoir, however, will supply timely information for readers who cannot dwell long upon the life and works of any one man.

The author gained his knowledge of Lowell from long personal intercourse, supplemented by information from the late Dr. Estes Howe, who married a sister of the poet's first wife, and from the late Robert Carter, Lowell's intimate friend, and co-editor of the brilliant and ill-fated *Pioneer*. Excepting the Biographical Sketch, before referred to, it is believed that no original account of Lowell has been published. That Sketch must have been the source — generally unacknowledged — from which most newspaper articles were drawn.

In September, 1891, while in Scotland, the author was asked to write an article upon Lowell for the *Contemporary Review*.

He wrote out of a full mind and memory, without the opportunity to consult books or old friends; and the article appeared a month later. That article, with additions and changes, forms the basis of the present Memoir. He did not make use of the Sketch, for in the course of years the point of view had changed.

It is announced that selections from Lowell's letters are about to appear, edited by his near friend and literary executor, Professor Charles Eliot Norton. The letters are sure to be full of interest; for Lowell showed consummate skill and tact in his correspondence, as in familiar talk with friends; and it would not be surprising if these volumes should become the most attractive part of his works.

Acknowledgments are due to Messrs. Houghton, Mifflin, & Co., for permission to copy the two poems, "The Foot Path," and "Beaver Brook."

CONTENTS

———◦◦◦———

3

CONTENTS

THE POET AND THE MAN

—••{✻⫶•——

I.

THE coming of a poet is an event, and
sometimes marks an epoch. A poet of original force does much to mould the thought
of his age, and to influence taste, sentiment,
and mental habitude. In ancient days his
songs kept alive the spirit of the clan while
marching to battle ; and in the intervals of
peace his ballads of love and war were the
delight of gentle and simple. The minstrel
has gone, along with knights, palmers, and
jesters, but in his place has come the printed
page, so that whoever will may take hold of
all that poets think and feel.

Poetry now envelops mankind as with an
atmosphere ; and who can estimate its influence ? Who can number the households
that have been cheered, sustained, and con-
soled by the verse of Longfellow and of
Bryant ? — the patriotic souls that have been

7

stirred by the "Union and Liberty" of
Holmes? — the youth whose aspirations
have been awakened by the appeals of
Whittier and Lowell?

A poet who is also a singer of the divine
love and good-will is the modern prophet;
he is the living voice of primitive Christianity. It is a noble gift to conceive forms
and ideas of beauty, but far more glorious
when piety, justice, and brotherhood are
themes of song; such poems may be
called, without irreverence, exemplars of
"the beauty of holiness."

Apart from his poetic genius, Lowell was
a grand man, and has left an example of
integrity, courage, and patriotism which
should endure. In the leading classes of
this country to-day the chief want is honesty; the chief vice, selfish greed. The
sense of honor which scorns unfair advantages in business, and trickery in politics,
seems to have almost disappeared. Money
and power are to be won, even if the whole
decalogue stands in the way. But a government of the people has no stable foundation
except in righteousness. Movements are
already felt, and when the lowest strata
heave, the highest must topple. The ur-
gent and immediate lesson for American

youth is that liberty never long survives
when truth and justice are dethroned.

If poets were produced as perfected
flowers are, their growth would be a fas-
cinating study.   And there are analogies.
Flowers have their times of expansion in
the life-giving sun, and of self-closure and
revery in the coolness of evening: they
reach upward to breathe all favoring influences, still holding fast by their roots to
mother earth; and when their calyces,
"each after his kind," unclose in varying
forms and colors, the glory of their being
is attained.   In thinking of the blossoms
of the ideal world it is natural, by comparison, to "consider the lilies," and to
wish that all the unfoldings of thought and
feeling were as simple and spontaneous as
theirs.
The student of poetry has a task unlike
the horticulturist's, for the latter knows
well the objects of his care: he antici-
pates their foliation and flowering; while
the budding poet often proves to be a
specimen of a new variety, not in the
books, and not to be classified by pedants.
Race, ancestry, education, and environ-
ment are all to be considered in the de-

velopment of a poet; and to know what
Lowell was it is necessary to consider the
leading facts of his life.

Few families in Massachusetts have
shown the persistent virility and the continually repeated high traits of character
which have marked the Lowells. They
are descended from Percival Lowell
(Lowle, it was anciently spelled), a mer-
chant of Bristol, England, who settled in
Newbury in 1639. Two or more of the
family were clergymen; and there is still
in the poet's house, Elmwood, Cambridge,
— the house in which he was born and in
which he died, — a panel taken from the an-
cestral home in Newbury, on which is represented a number of clergymen, seated
at a table with long clay pipes, but no
decanters, engaged in friendly discussion.
On the pictured wall is seen this motto:
*In necessariis unitas; in non necessariis liber-
tas; in omnibus caritas.* The panel is a
rude specimen of art, but rich in suggestion.

In each generation the family has furnished distinguished men and public ben-
efactors. John Lowell, the poet's grand-
father, an eminent legislator and judge,
drafted the clause in the Constitution of
Massachusetts (1820) which put an end

to slavery in the State. The poet was prouder of this honor than he would have been of a patent of nobility. Another of the family was the chief promoter of cotton manufacture in the city which bears his name. Another founded the Lowell Institute which furnishes free lectures in Boston.

The poet's father, Rev. Charles Lowell, D. D., was for more than half a century minister of the West Church in Boston: but he lived in Cambridge, four miles distant, in a house built by the last representative of British authority in the Province; namely, Peter Oliver, stamp distributer, who, having been waited upon "by a committee of about four thousand," had resigned his function and left the country. Dr. Lowell was universally respected and beloved. Like his ancestors and collateral relatives, he was a man of solid and practical ability, and had little in common with some of his imaginative and versatile children. His father, Judge John Lowell, when a youth of seventeen furnished a part of the *Pietas et Gratulatio*, a wonderful round-robin, partly in Latin, sent by Harvard College in 1761 to King George III. The evidence of the heavy heroics would not be sufficient to convict him of being

a poet; and it is probable that James and
Robert, his grandsons, were the first of the
family to write spontaneous verse.

Dr. Lowell's wife was Harriet Traill
Spence, born in Portsmouth, N. H., the
daughter of an officer in the United States
Navy, who was descended from an Orkney
family, and possibly from Sir Patrick
Spens. The poet often fondly referred to
the well-known ballad, and was fain to
think that its hero might have been one of
his far-away ancestors. It was from his
mother, who was certainly of Scottish, and
probably of Celtic, blood, that he inherited
his passionate love of poetry, and especially of the old ballads.

Dr. Lowell died in 1861. For many
years previous he had been a widower and
lived with his son James. Though nomi-
nally minister, he rarely preached, but
made occasional parochial visits, and gave
his leisure to reading. Memory brings to
mind a slender and (rather grimly) handsome man; the ellipse of his lean face and
high forehead fringed with gray hair; his
eyes steady and not unkind; his voice deep
and metallic ; his manner grave. Intelli-,
gence, veracity, and firmness shone in that
striking countenance, but no sparkle of

the humor or the lively genius of his famous
son. The highest and noblest traits of
our race — probity, justice, and honor —
were his; and so sensitive was he that
when his eldest son, who was engaged in
business, became involved in debt, he vol-
untarily parted with a sum of money that
would have made most fathers pause.
This son was the father of two youths who
died in the War of the Rebellion; youths
whose fate was the subject of the most pathetic and inspired passage in Lowell's
poems.[1]

Dr. Lowell's second son, Robert Traill
Spence Lowell, was an author and poet of
mark, a clergyman in the Episcopal Church,
and latterly a professor in Union College,
Schenectady, N.Y., where he died in 1891,
not long after his younger brother. The
subject of this memoir used to relate with
glee, and doubtless with picturesque exag-
eration, the story of an encounter which
took place when the new priest first came
home on a visit after the (so-called) apos-
tasy. The father had ransacked his antique theological armory, and with the un-
conscious gravity of Don Quixote shivered
lances for Congregationalism and against

[1] " Biglow Papers," Second Series, Letter x., Stanzas 15, 16, 17.

the Apostolic Succession, and gesticulated
over the great parchment-covered quartos
with which the floor was strewed.   Still, the
good doctor, when in his pulpit, preached
only practical Christianity, and never doc-
trinal sermons.   This story gives a hint of
a possible likeness between the old Christian knight and the *Rev. Homer Wilbur.*

The doctor's eldest daughter, Mrs. Putnam, who is (1893) still living, is an able
woman, a writer of historical and political
essays.   Her only son, Captain William
Lowell Putnam, just from college, beautiful as a young Apollo, and full of promise, was killed at Ball's Bluff early in the
war.   The three slain nephews of the poet
were the only males of the generation following him.[1]

An unmarried sister, Rebecca, very re-
tiring in her ways, died before the poet
became widely known.   It will be seen
that there were three sons and two daughters.   Of the five children the poet was
the youngest, and was born on Washington's Birthday, Feb. 22, 1819.

If poetic genius is smothered by luxury,
it is as surely pinched and starved by pov-

---

[1] See the touching dedication, prefixed to the "Commemoration Ode."

erty. The family was in comfortable circumstances; the father was prudent and saving, and the children, though brought up in old-fashioned simplicity, never knew want. The house counted for much in the family happiness. It is sombre and without architectural beauty, but spacious and comfortable. It is set in an ample grassy field near Mount Auburn, just away from the travelled road, and is surrounded by tall, thick sheltering trees and flowering shrubs. It is a fit retreat for a dreamer or philosopher, since no sound breaks the stillness except that of the wind in the pine boughs, and the songs of the many birds that lodge in the thick coverts. The place which this garden held in the poet's mind is shown in many poems and essays.

The library contained between three and four thousand volumes, including an excellent collection of English and French classics in best editions, also travels, plays, stories, and biographies, the pick of some centuries, known and loved by the fraternity of lettered men. In this rare library Dr. Lowell's children had free range, and to it the poet in later years made many additions, including German, Italian, and Spanish masterpieces. This was his real

education. He attended a good private
school, and entered Harvard College in his
sixteenth year; but he was a lagging student, indifferent to reproof, and at last
was rusticated. The place of his rustica-
tion was Concord, and he refers to it in
the " Biglow Papers ": [1]

> " I know the village, though: was sent there once
> A-schoolin', cause to home I played the dunce."

He was still in banishment when the course
was ending; and it is said he saw the out-
door festivities of his class through a rift
in the cover of a wagon in which he had
surreptitiously returned. He had written
verse while in college, and had been chosen
class-poet, but, as the authorities refused
to remit his sentence, the poem was printed
and was not read by its author.

Lowell often spoke of this, but without
·bitterness; he felt that the action of the
faculty was just. He said to the writer
that while in college he was in the habit
of reading all the books he came across,
excepting those prescribed for his course of
study, and that he was sure he would never
have been allowed to take his degree if he
had not been his father's son. He la-

[1] Mason and Slidell, Second Series.

mented this early perverseness, because
there remained so much more to do before
he could become a scholar.   Still his brilliant qualities were manifest from the first,
and students and professors alike predicted
for him a distinguished career.

Meantime, in his father's library he came
to know every rood in the long highway
of English literature, besides making some
excursions in foreign territory.   He had
the prescience of genius, and assimilated
all his eager eyes fell upon and his instinctive judgment approved.   He read all
manner of out-of-the-way things; and it
was seldom in his maturer years that a
book was named of which he did not know
something.

II. •

LOWELL came into the world in a fortunate time; the reaction against Puritan rule, with its narrowness and illiberality, was well under way. Thought was free. The treasures of the classics were opened. Not only the fathers of Greek and Latin poetry, but Dante and Shakespeare, had been rediscovered. Scholarship was getting extricated from pedantry. New ideas in poetry and philosophy were brought from Germany by returning students. Science was preparing for its great and beneficent career. With the new era the college and the region were becoming a recognized part of the realm of letters and art. This was the beginning of the fruitful period of American literature, as well as of humanitarian philosophy and of boundless social improvement.[1] In that time began to appear the poems of Bryant, Longfellow, Holmes, and Whittier, the essays of Chan-

[1] See " The Awakening of New England," in *Contemporary Review* for August, 1888.

ning and Emerson, and the histories of Bancroft and Prescott.

It was fortunate also for Lowell that what was quaint, picturesque, and characteristic in the old life had not wholly disappeared. Perhaps it is partly due to the haze of distance, but there is something idyllic,— some tinge of romance, — as one looks back upon the rural Yankee of sixty years ago, when men's faces and speech had not become as like as pebbles. We know that the old life did not seem in the least picturesque to those who lived it. All martyrdoms, it has been said, looked mean when they were suffered, and the poetic side of struggles and endurance is dimly perceived until events have become history. In Lowell's youth the provincial period seemed near. In his essay, "Cambridge Thirty Years Ago," published in 1853, he tells us that "old women, capped and spectacled, still peered through the same windows from which they had watched Lord Percy's artillery rumble by to Lexington, or caught a glimpse of the handsome Virginian general who had come to wield our Saxon chivalry." Plenty of people in Cambridge spoke the old, rustic, chimney-corner English now becoming ex-

tinct. The home-life, the dress and manners of the elders had not changed greatly
from the time of Bunyan. The accompaniments of the College Commencement and
of the militia trainings were for the popu-
lace what Bartlemy Fair was for Londoners.
Those festivals kept alive the traditions of
the old times, as well as the bucolic speech,
with its billowy inflections and its nasal
tone. In the part of Cambridge near
Boston called "the Port," observers like
Holmes and Lowell could take an account
of the commerce of the period,— a commerce not in goods and wares only, but in
jokes, stories, pranks, and rustic repartee.
In the essay already cited Lowell says,
"Great white-topped wagons, each drawn
by double files of six or eight horses, with
its dusty bucket swinging from the hinder
axle, and its grim bull-dog trotting silent
underneath, . . . brought all the wares
and products of the country to their mart
and seaport in Boston. These filled the
inn-yards, or were ranged side by side
under broad-roofed sheds; and far into
the night the mirth of their lusty drivers
clamored from the red-curtained bar-room,
while the single lantern, swaying to and
fro in the black cavern of the stables, made

a Rembrandt of the group of hostlers and horses below."

Teaming continued to be carried on by those great wagons until within the memory of the writer.

From such reminiscences we see the source of our poet's knowledge of Yankee life and character, and his familiarity with the dialect. A man born since 1850 could not have written a page of the "Biglow Papers," nor told the inimitable "Fitz Adam's Story." That old time has gone by. It would be difficult to find, except in remote and unfrequented settlements, any survival of the customs and speech which Lowell has so vividly depicted; so that the dialect of the "Biglow Papers" has become almost obsolete to the younger generation of readers.

Carlyle observes that every day is at the convergence of two eternities, past and to come; but it is important for the poet that the convergence for him occurs upon an epoch of change. Behind the youthful Lowell was the vanishing age of the rustic Yankee, with its audacious and far-glancing wit and its delicious quaintness of phrase; while before him was an idealization of memory and the beginning of a new

era of song. Happily for the world, the
subjects of his humorous and satiric verse
had not all gone into darkness before his
inspiration and power came.

But the poetical career was not to begin
at once. Various symptoms had shown
the anxious father that the Benjamin of
the family was addicted to rhyming, and
he was inclined to connect this folly with
his son's indolence. So after many exhor-
tations, and perhaps tears, he exacted a
promise from the young man that he would
make no more verses, but betake himself
to serious study. The law was chosen,—
a common resource when a student has no
vocation for anything,— and after some two
years the degree of LL. B. was achieved.
Practice, however, has small connection with
theory; and it was evident from Lowell's
story, "My First Client" that his practice
was a good joke. Notes scribbled on the
waste paper of his desk began to take met-
rical form. The renunciation of the Muses
did not hold, and would not hold, as the
father could not fail to see. Pegasus was
restive harnessed to a cart.

But a warning should be interposed.

" ' Tis not the singer's wish that makes the song."

The youth who dabbles in verse generally deceives himself.   Young pretender!
if you have to *seek* poetic phrase and rhyme,
stop!   The tripod of the ancient oracle
was not worked by a pump.   But if the
Muse seeks you, follows you, haunts you,
you will not stop; you cannot.

Another development was in progress.
From a gay youth, fond of chaffing, and
ready to jeer at abolitionists, Lowell became a reformer and a devotee to spiritual
life.   No more complete renunciation of
the "world" was ever made, as succeeding
years were to show; and it was not an easy
thing for a favorite of fortune, especially
for one with such a buoyant nature.   Love
was the agent in this conversion.   He had
become enamoured of Miss Maria White, a
young lady of rare beauty and noble character.   She wrote poems of unusual merit,
and one of them, "The Alpine Sheep," is
widely known.   Chiefly she was devoted to
the anti-slavery cause, and made her influence felt.   The change on the part of
Lowell was not the passing whim of a
lover, but became the steadfast purpose of
a man.   He came to see that slavery was
a contradiction and lie in the constitution
of a free country, and from that time

his best efforts were devoted to its over-throw.

Too much stress should not be laid upon the good influence exerted by Miss White. The main features of Lowell's character were predestined, and its legitimate development could not have been long delayed. Miss White was young, not to say immature, — a being all delicacy, purity, and ideality. Under the light of her steadfast eyes worldly illusions fell. To be near her was to live in an atmosphere of moral beauty. Such was the influence which moved her lover,— an influence of which neither was fully conscious.

In his twenty-second year his first volume of verse was published: "A Year's Life." Love is naturally its theme, — love, liberty, and lofty ideals. The collection has not been reprinted as a whole, but some of the pieces have been preserved in the complete edition of his poems.

Shortly after, in collaboration with his friend Robert Carter, he edited *The Pioneer*, a monthly magazine for which the American public was not ready. The first number contained two short stories by Hawthorne, poems by Mrs. Browning, Poe, Whittier, and Lowell, and articles by John

S. Dwight, William W. Story, and others. Seldom was richer freight intrusted to a poet's argosy. The magazine came to an end after the third number. Probably the publisher's want of business qualities and experience was as decisive as the lack of public appreciation; but the literary taste of the United States in 1844 is not recalled with much pride.

He was married in that year to the lady just mentioned, and shortly after was published a second volume, in which were manifest maturer power and a more masculine freedom of touch. While his devotion to his love grew more tender, he saw the world in a new light. He sang of the wrongs of the poor and the slave; of the emptiness of life without conviction; the nullity of poetry without noble purpose; the vapidness of preaching without piety; the shame of law without justice; the blank horror of a world without God. As time went on he learned to purify his style, and gain a surer mastery of expression, but this early impulse ceased only with his life. Some of these poems glow with the beautiful enthusiasm of youth; they give hope for uplifting the fallen; they rebuke the strife of sects with parables of Christian love. The most vigorous of these is "The Present Crisis," passages from which have been repeated by public speakers ever since. Were it not for an incongruous figure in the final couplet, this would be an ideal prophetic poem.

But, at the time when they appeared, such a view of Lowell's early poems would have been received with almost universal derision. Before 1850 an ordinary Bostonian, as well as most people "in society," would have said, if inquired of, that Lowell was a hare-brained fellow with some knack at verse-making, — a friend of fanatics and come-out-ers, like Abby Folsom and Father Lamson, a man out of touch with the world, and a dreamer of Utopian dreams. And, so much is the judgment controlled by personal prejudice, few critics were disposed to consider his claims as a poet. He was more frequently pooh-poohed than praised, and his books had very few buyers. It would have greatly astonished the exalted society in which Everett, Ticknor, Prescott, Hillard, and Harvard professors moved, if it had been foretold that this long-haired youth, who consorted with Garrison and other impossible folk, and sat without shame

with women-orators and freed slaves upon
public platforms, would in forty years be
one of the most distinguished of Americans, a satirist and poet of world-wide fame;
one òf the few great writers of brilliant and
learned prose, and the most honored of
foreign ministers.

It may be well here at the outset to take
a look at him and his wife. The portraits
of this pair of idealists painted by William
Page still hang in the sombre entrance hall
at Elmwood; she, with refined features,
transparent skin, starry blue eyes, and
smooth bands of light brown hair; he, with
serious face and eyes in shadow; with
ruddy, wavy, and glossy auburn hair, falling
almost to the shoulders, a full reddish
beard, wearing a coarse-textured brown coat
and a broad linen collar turned carelessly
down. There are few modern portraits in
which costume counts for so little, and soul
for so much. In Page's time the poet's eyes
and forehead, though suggestive of great
possibilities, were calm as a boy's; the forbidding wrinkles and nervous contractions
between and above the eyebrows, shown
in more recent portraits, were the results
of the long and painful studies of later
years.

It was a time of productiveness as well as bliss. Literatures were explored, though discursively, sketches were made, and poems born. There would have been little in life to ask, but for the increasing fragility of his wife, and the early death of their children. Of four or five born in their nine years of wedlock only one survived.[1] The plainly dressed couple, at whose Titianesque portraits we have just looked, lived very simply, and wholly apart from the fashionable world. They were devoted to each other and to all good works, looking for the speedy coming of truth and righteousness. Generous and beautiful illusion! How dark the world would be to young hearts, if they were to see it as after three-score it appears to be! There was a season just before the upheavals of 1848 when an ardent faith was in the air, especially with abolitionists and other spiritually minded people. They were confident that slavery, poverty, and crime were to disappear, and human brotherhood was to create a new heaven upon earth. It was to this end that the poetry and the daily aspirations of Lowell tended. It is said that at one period, with the intent of

[1] Mrs. Edward Burnett.

doing away with social distinctions, the old family servants were bidden to the table of the master and mistress; but this was soon felt to be an inconvenience, and the custom did not long continue.

His love of nature was an absorbing passion, and led him to make excursions in all the region about Cambridge. He followed the silver windings of the Charles, and mused under the spreading willows; he roamed through the fringe of woods about Fresh Pond; he climbed the heights of Belmont, or loitered among the Waverley oaks, — huge trees of unknown age, which stand as if grouped for a Corôt, — or wandered along Beaver Brook, whose pretty cascade and ruined mill are souvenirs of one of his most perfect poems; or, more frequently still, he lingered among the wooded knolls of the neighboring cemetery, destined to be his final resting-place.

When out for a walk nothing escaped him, — not the plumage of a bird, the leafage of a tree, the color of a blossom, nor a trait upon a human countenance. He knew almost every bird by its note, its color, and its flight. He knew where flowers grew, and when they should appear. All this knowledge might have been pos-

sessed by some observer with little sentiment, but it was with eyes of love that
Lowell looked upon the world. It is a
beautiful touch in one of his dialect poems
where he says, —

> "An' th' airth don't git put out with me
> That love her 's though she was a woman:
> Why th' ain't a bird upon a tree
> But half forgives my bein' human."

In later years he made more distant
trips, to Moosehead Lake and to the Adi-
rondacks, where (in company with Agassiz,
Wyman, Emerson, Howe, and Stillman)
he met lumbermen, trappers, and deer-
stalkers, and came to know —

> "The shy, wood-wandering brood of Character."

III.

THE war with Mexico (1846) was brought
on for the purpose of gaining new territory
for the extension of slavery. The action
of Polk's administration was looked upon
with shame and anger by most Northern
men. No one was deceived by the base
official declaration that war existed by the
act of Mexico; yet from various motives
of interest,— political, personal, and "religious," nearly all influential people continued to oppose the agitation of the
question of slavery, — the cause of the war
and of most of the troubles of the time.

Lowell was one day in a lawyer's office
in Court Square, Boston, when there was
heard without the unusual sound of fife
and drum. It soon appeared that it was
a call for volunteers for a Massachusetts
regiment, and the poet's quick indignation rose; but his good sense and native
humor soon got the better of his wrath.
His friends in the office, one of whom re-

lated the incident to the writer,[1] long remembered the keen light in his eyes, and his caustic comments upon the humiliating scene. A few days later in the *Boston Courier* appeared anonymously the first poem of *Hosea Biglow*, introduced with grave and felicitous humor by *Rev. Homer Wilbur*, delighting the anti-slavery party, and gradually setting the whole Northern people in crepitating chuckles of laughter. It was as in France where once an epigram might shake a throne. Men upon whom the inflexible logic of Garrison was wasted, who had listened unmoved to the matchless eloquence of Wendell Phillips, and read with indifference the burning verse of Whittier, gave in without parley to this new assault. Every one felt that this ballad embodied the common-sense, the religious convictions, the Puritan *grit*, and the humane feelings of the North. The concentrated energy was resistless. But it was something more; the sharp thrusts in rustic phrase, the native wit, and the irony which played upon the lines, making them like live electric wires, produced a combination of mirth and conviction that was wholly new. Unlike the unheeded logic,

[1] Judge Robert I. Burbank.

eloquence, and burning verse, the comic and catching rhymes went everywhere as on wings; and while men repeated the drolleries the deeper import sank into their hearts. Other poems followed, a running fire of sarcasm hard to bear. As the war went on the position of its Northern supporters became pitiable.

It seems strange to remember that Sumner, while he praised the points made by the then unknown Yankee poet, regretted that the ballad had not been written *in English.* But Sumner had no sense of humor, and did not see that not only the comedy, but the argument, gained force from the dialect. Thus, to say the New Testament teaches that war is wrong, is not a very startling proposition; but when *Hosea* says,—

" We kind o' thought Christ went ag'in war an' pillage,
     An' thet eppylets wern't the best mark of a saint,"

the sidelong irony offers to the adversary a cutting edge instead of a handle.

The parson, too, is by no means an unimportant character, being a delightful and necessary complement to his irrepressible parishioner and *protégé,* He has the high sense of honor and ingenuousness of *Colonel Newcome*, a little of the serious whimsicality of *Don Quixote*, and a trace of an old-fashioned preacher's pedantry and prosiness. He is strong in quotation from unexpected sources, and often makes an apt stroke. He is distinctly a humorous character.

Wit and humor are often confounded, and as often bunglingly defined. Landor says, "Who ever has humor has wit, although it does not follow that who ever has wit has humor. Humor is wit appertaining to character, and indulges in breadth of drollery, rather than in play and brilliancy of point." Wit sparkles and explodes in fireworks; humor is exuberant, consistent in inconsistency, causing an easy ripple of mirth. Wit is more common than humor, for humor is an attribute of genius. Lowell's creations are humorous, though some of them scatter witticisms like rice at a wedding.

"The Biglow Papers" is like no other book; the comedy begins with the title-page, and overruns the index. "The Notices of an Independent Press" are delightful burlesques of the methods of certain newspaper reviewers. The prefaces, notes, and comments are in perfect keeping; serious in one view, jocose in another: there is a back-handed stroke in them all. It is not risking much to say that it is the wittiest and best-sustained satire in English.

When the book was being printed there was a vacant page which it was thought should be filled. (For that space Lowell wrote off-hand the now famous ballad of "'The Courtin'," containing six stanzas, printed as an excerpt from a supposititious newspaper notice. In a subsequent edition he added six more, and in the collected poems there are twenty-four. Though the first sketch contained the substance, yet the added stanzas so fill out and heighten the picture that not one of them can be pronounced superfluous. This ballad may be regarded as a trifle by some, but it is a Flemish picture of manners and speech in the last generation, exquisite in feeling and treatment; in fact, one of those miraculous trifles in which the comic and tender elements are vitally blended; which only genius creates, and which the hearts of mankind will forever preserve. We may smile at *Huldy* and *Zekel*, but their Courtin' is a repetition of the world-old drama, the same in palace as in farm-house, to which no son or daughter of Eve can be indifferent.

To this period of exaltation and exuberance belongs "The Vision of Sir Launfal," based upon one of the legends of King Arthur's knights. Any summary of the beautiful story would be a profanation; it is enough to say that it is a lesson of brotherly love set in a parable of holy beauty. The prelude of the first part is a description of the sights, sounds, and odors of springtime in New England; of the second, the keen splendors of our Northern winter. The spring prelude is all movement and ecstasy, and came to the poet in a happy hour when he had only to dip his pen in ink. Passages from this are continually appearing in the newspapers; young editors rediscover it, and must forthwith display specimens. The whole poem is the overflow of a full heart, and its composition occupied less than two days, during which he scarcely ate or slept. It is by far the most popular of his serious poems.

"A Fable for Critics" purports to be a view of a procession of American, authors defiling before Apollo. It follows in plan Leigh Hunt's mild "Feast of Poets,"—

but with a difference. The title-page, in black and red, tells us that it was —

" Set forth in October, the 21st day,
   In the year '48. G. P. Putnam, Broadway.

The rhymed preface prepares us to follow a masked harlequin in a frolic. Never in the New World was there a parallel instance of exultant audacity. It is the gay humor of a youth in the freedom of an anonymous pasquinade, — revelling in puns, clashing unexpected and all-but-impossible rhymes like cymbals, tossing off grotesque epithets and comparisons, and going in a break-neck canter, like that of a race-horse let loose. And yet, underneath the fun and riot, we find outline portraits and swift estimates which, though not always wholly just, are of marvellous acuteness and force. Some of the sketches, — for instance, those of Emerson, Parker, Willis, Hawthorne and Whittier, — in their general faithfulness and power of discrimination, are the most lifelike miniatures ever made of these men. The sharp and philosophic discrimination between Emerson and Carlyle, done so long ago as 1848, and by a youth of twenty-nine, is something to think of. The uproar raised by lesser authors, who were omitted, and by friends of Margaret Fuller, who was thought to be lampooned as *Miranda*, subsided in time; and to-day most critics agree that this early satirical view of American literature was singularly just and prophetic, and that its hard hits and sharp reproofs were salutary.   Its main counsel is to avoid imitation of foreign models, to be true to the ideas of the democratic New World, to be independent in thought and modest in expression, and to wait for the development of a worthy literature and art at home.   Excepting "The Biglow Papers" and "The Vision of Sir Launfal," this poem is probably more read in the United States than any production of Lowell's.   Many of his admirers know it by heart.

In the same year were published two volumes of collected poems.

He visited Europe in 1851, accompanied by his wife, and returned the following year.   Her health had long been failing, and she died in the autumn of 1853.

After her death he printed (privately) a small memorial volume of her poems, with a photographic copy of the beautiful portrait by William Page which has been mentioned.

On the day of her death a daughter was born to Longfellow, whose house was not far from Elmwood, and the double incident was the subject of one of the most imaginative and exquisite of his minor poems. " The Two Angels."

" 'T was at thy door, O friend ! and not at mine,
The angel with the amaranthine wreath,
Pausing, descended, and with voice divine
Whispered a word that had a sound like Death.

Then fell upon the house a sudden gloom,
A shadow on those features fair and thin;
And softly, from that hushed and darkened room,
Two angels issued, where but one went in."

IV.

FOR some years between 1853 and 1859, Lowell received a few of his Cambridge friends on Sunday afternoons in his study, a front room in the third story. On Friday evenings there was another gathering, ostensibly for whist, at the house of each of the party in turn. Of those who were members of the whist-club, Dr. Estes Howe, Robert Carter, Henry Ware, and Lowell are dead; the survivors are John Holmes, John Bartlett, and the present writer. In social meetings Lowell was naturally the leading spirit, and the one whose talk no one was willing to miss; yet he was never the imperious Johnson of the club; every one had his chance. The conversation took a wide range over literature and art, as well as the field of politics, on which lines of battle were forming, then little suspected. In the tranquil, peace-loving North "coming events" did not "cast their shadows before."

At the period following his great loss

he was naturally sobered, but still generally cheerful, and sometimes momentarily
gay. His habitual manner had a mellow,
autumnal glow. His serious conversation
was suggestive and inspiring, and a sense
of uplifting followed, as from seeing a play
of Shakespeare, or hearing a symphony of
Beethoven. But it was impossible for him
to repress the bright fancies and droll con-
ceits suggested by reading and conversation. Wit was as natural to him as breath-
ing, and when the mood was on he could not
help seeing and signalling puns. But epigrams and puns were the accompaniments,
and not the end and aim of his conversation:
his perceptions were keen and just; his
reading had been well-nigh universal; and,
with his instant power of comparison, his
judgments were like intuitions. But his
discourse often took on an airy and tanta-
lizing form, and wreathed itself in irony,
or flowered in simile, or exploded in arti-
fices, until it ended in some merry absurd-
ity. Such play of argument, fancy, humor,
word-twisting, and sparkling nonsense was
seldom witnessed, except in the talk of the
Autocrat of the Breakfast Table. At the
whist-table, when he was in a flow of spirits,
the deal was often interrupted by his

audacious inventions, his deft touches in dressing a story, his assumption of Yankee shrewdness or clownishness, or his mimicry of antique pedants. Sometimes he would *assume* an imaginary character, and sustain it during an evening. Once when a member's birthday fell on the day of the club's meeting, Lowell preceded the guest to the supper-room, walking backward, holding a pair of great silver candlesticks, and bowing, like a lord-chamberlain ushering a king.

Before he had become worn with study his face was usually radiant with smiles. His eyes were searching at times, but benevolent, especially to people of low degree. A servant in the writer's house who had admitted Lowell one evening, said to her mistress in naïve admiration, " I declare, ma'am, Mr. Lowell has the *coaxinest* eyes I ever see wid a man."

At that period he was nearing the acme of his powers.

His passion for nature was kept alive by walks in surrounding country, and by occasional trips to aboriginal forests. It was the time of anemones, cardinal flowers, bobolinks, robins, and cat-birds; of Maine lakes and Adirondack forests; of Arthurian legends, and idyls of Huldah and Zekel. These by and by were to give way to the exhausting study of Dante, to the burden of criticism and the production of poems like "The Cathedral." He was lithe, mobile, and impressionable in mind and body, and at his best for the enjoyment of life and for the delight of friends.

As an abolitionist or free-soiler he was in no danger of being lionized. "Society" in Boston and Cambridge forgave no friend of the slave until long after; and at that time Lowell seldom met any but near relatives or old friends. But there was a natural reaction against some of the austere habits of former years. The coarse-textured brown coat of the Page portrait was no longer worn, the size of the linen collar was retrenched, and the auburn locks were shorter, though carefully kept. A velvet jacket was in common use indoors, and never man lived who was more fastidious in the details of the toilet. All things were in harmony with a refined and delicate nature. One might as soon expect to find a smirch on the petals of a new Easter lily as upon his linen or hands. Trifles, but significant. A photograph exists, taken in 1854 or 1855, in which he is rep-

resented sitting with his face partly in
profile. The hair is long (according to
modern notions), falling in soft waves, and
completely covering the ears. The face
appears tranquil when viewed at a distance, but on closer inspection there is
perceived a subtle smile of which the lines
are as elusive as those around the mouth of
da Vinci's *La Gioconda*. Two of his friends
of the whist-club had gone with him to the
photographer's; some good stories were
told, and the picture shows that the gleam
of fun had scarcely left the sitter's face.
This curious, flickering expression was
somehow lost in the engraving afterwards
made from the picture.

In 1854 Lowell delivered a course of
twelve lectures on the British Poets at the
Lowell Institute. They were not printed
at the time, except partially, in newspaper
reports, but doubtless many of their ideas
were absorbed in the published essays. In
these lectures the qualities of his prose
style began to be manifest. It was felt by
every hearer to be the prose of a poet, as
it teemed with original images, fortunate
epithets, and artistically wrought allusions,
and had a movement and music all its own.
A few friends from Cambridge attended

these lectures, walking into the city, and more than once in deep snow. The lecturer humorously acknowledged his indebtedness to them, saying that when he saw their faces he was in presence of his literary conscience. These lectures have not been published as yet, and may not be.

In 1855, Longfellow having resigned his place as professor of modern languages and literature in Harvard College, Lowell was appointed his successor, with leave of absence, that he might perfect himself in his studies. He went to Germany, passing most of his time at Dresden, but did not remain so long as he had intended. In later years he gave an amusing explanation of his premature return; and the story, perhaps, is not unworthy of being repeated, as it is the thistle-downs of humor which are apt to be blown away from stately biographies. Lowell told the story at a whist-party. "I had given instructions," he said, "to my bankers in London to notify me when my balance was reduced to a certain sum; and then I settled myself to my studies, keeping no account of the drafts I drew from time to time. I supposed I had still a good sum to the fore, and a pleasant time in prospect; but I was surprised one day to receive notice that my account had touched the figure I had mentioned. There was nothing to do but pack up and go home, which I did. Mark the sequel! Some years afterward I received a letter from the bankers, stating that owing to the error of a clerk I had been charged with a draft for so-and-so-many pounds, which ought to have been debited to the account of a kinsman of mine; and that sum, with compound interest, was subject to my order. They regretted the inconvenience I had suffered by the shortening of my visit, and, by way of compensation, they suggested an investment — if I did not need the money at once — which they thought would turn out well. I thanked them and asked them to invest the money as they thought best. Well, in a year I got a draft for near £700. With that I refurnished my house. Now you, who are always preaching figures, and Poor Richard, and business habits, what do you say to *that?* If I had kept an account and known how it stood, *I should have spent that money*, and you would not now be sitting in those easy-chairs, or walking on a Wilton carpet. No, hang accounts and figures!"

Before the laughter subsided, Dr. Estes Howe (his brother-in-law) said he was able to add a story which would further illustrate Lowell's original financial methods. Said the doctor, "James, as you know, has some good apple-trees; and a few years ago he made a quantity of cider, and then set about looking for bottles. He found a good number and filled them, but still there was a surplus of cider. So what did he do, but ask half a dozen friends to supper, send in to Parker's for the 'feed,' and to Pierce's for a case of champagne, merely to get bottles for that cider!"

This was Lowell's airy way in early life, when at leisure; and this characteristic trait cannot be omitted in any account of him. But all things had their turn. After a period of indolence he would take to his desk, where he "toiled terribly." In serious talk he was as strenuous as any of his Puritan ancestors. To the world he was courteous, but reserved, with a due mingling of dignity; to inferiors, especially generous and considerate; to the vulgar and presuming, a glacier; to his family and near friends, the most delightful and sunshiny being that ever came from the Author of joy.

V.

THE *Atlantic Monthly* was started in the autumn of 1857. It was the project of a young enthusiast, who desired to bring the literary influence of New England to aid the anti-slavery cause. Four years before (1853), the magazine was to have been undertaken by the publisher of "Uncle Tom's Cabin;" but when all things appeared to be ready he changed his mind and declined to go on. For that magazine Lowell sent his poem "The Oriole's Nest." After that the projector continued his conferences and correspondence with leading writers, and, the due co-operation having been secured, the firm of Phillips, Sampson, & Co., was finally induced to become the publishers. The influence which brought this about came largely from Mrs. Stowe, who saw Mr. Phillips almost daily, and from Mr. William Lee, a junior member of the firm. The projector, who then lived in Cambridge, naturally consulted his neighbors, Lowell and

The Oriole's Nest.

~~Then~~ May.

1

When oaken woods with buds are pink
And new birds every morning sing;
When pickle they upon the brink
Pauses & knows not which to fling,
Whether fresh bud & bloom again,
Or hoarfrost silvering hill & plain;

2

Then from the honeysuckle gray
The oriole, with experienced quest,
Twitches the fibrous bark away,
The cordage of his hammock-nest,
Nor fails by times to pour a note
Rich as the orange of his throat.

The stanzas in fac simile are from a poem first entitled
"The Oriole's Nest." The MSS. in possession of the author
bear the date of 1853.

Longfellow. It is not to be understood that it was ever intended to make the magazine *an organ*, or that it should be, except occasionally, a vehicle of anti-slavery doctrine. At that time literary periodicals in the United States were professedly neutral, but most were really subservient to pro-slavery interests. The bulk of the matter of the new magazine was to be literary and not controversial; but it was intended there should be frequent political articles to indicate its purpose. That purpose was to be the point of the arrow, or rather the ram of the ship; and all the tug of the sails, and all the power of the screw, were to give it impetus.

While public opinion and fashionable society were hostile, Garrison and Phillips preached in vain; the new project was to enlist society and opinion upon the righteous side, by the combination of all the men of genius whom the public honored and loved. It succeeded. The new magazine made an impression from the first, and voices that had once hooted at the early abolitionists applauded the new combination of genius with moral purpose. The projector had come to Boston with that idea, and toiled for years to carry it out.

The leading authors invited to contribute,
— eleven of them, — with two members of
the firm of publishers (Mr. Phillips and Mr.
Wyman), and one person who represented
both publishers and authors (leading an
amphibious existence between the two),
met at a dinner to agree upon prelimina-
ries. At that dinner the projector, having
previously sounded Lowell, rose without
a suggestion from any person, and without
the knowledge of any person, — author or
publisher, — and nominated Lowell as ed-
itor-in-chief. He himself served as the
assistant editor, received and answered
the letters, and gave the first reading to
all the myriads of contributions.

Lowell was not methodical, and he hated
routine work; but he applied himself stren-
uously, and gave a high tone to the magazine. His own contributions were good,
and often brilliant, but were not to be
compared in general interest with the fortunate stroke of Holmes. At the dinner
just mentioned Lowell said, "I will take
the place, as you all seem to think I should;
but, if success is achieved, we shall owe
it mainly to the doctor." He continued
(talking to the present writer) his observa-
tions upon Holmes, in which he showed

himself a psychological observer, and something of a prophet: —

"You see, the doctor is like a bright mountain stream that has been dammed up among the hills, and is waiting for an outlet into the Atlantic." (The name of the magazine was suggested by Holmes.) "You will find he has a wonderful store of thoughts, — serious, comic, pathetic, and poetic, — of comparisons, figures, and illustrations. I have seen nothing of his preparation, but I imagine he is ready. It will be something wholly new, and his reputation as a prose-writer will date from this magazine."

These are not Lowell's words, but they contain the substance of what he said.

For two years or more the monthly dinners of the *Atlantic* contributors occurred on the day of publication. They were generally at Parker's, but one was at Fontarive's in Winter Place, and one at Porter's in North Cambridge. It is a misfortune that no notes were kept of the table-talk. The gatherings were memorable, and would have been memorable in any city of the world.

The bright, powerful, and inspired faces that surrounded the ellipse come to mind almost like a sight of yesterday. Each guest in turn seems to fix his eyes upon the on-looker in this miraculous camera. The group is immortal; the separate faces so many varying expressions of genius. Brilliant lights and softly luminous shades seem to play around the table, until the colors and forms are mingled as in the heart of a picture by Turner. There was Holmes in the flush of his new fame as the Autocrat,—a man whose genius flamed out in his speech and expression, as clearly as in his original and sparkling works. There was Lowell, with features of singular power, and eyes which dazzled and charmed. In merriment he was irresistible; in higher moods his face shone like a soul made visible. There was Emerson, thoughtful, but shrewdly observant, and with the placid look of an optimistic philosopher, whose smile was a benediction; Longfellow, with a head which Phidias might have modelled, by turns calm or radiant, seldom speaking, but always using the fit word; Agassiz, glowing with good humor, simple in phrase and massive in intellect; Whittier, with noble head and deep-set, brilliant eyes, grown spare and taciturn from ill-health, an ascetic at table, eager only for intellectual enjoyment; Quincy, with patrician air, curious learning, and felicity in epigram; Dwight, with the sky-reaching architecture of Beethoven's symphonies in his brain; Felton, Greek to his fingers' ends, happy in wise discourse and in Homeric laughter; Motley, stateliest man of his time, just about to depart for Europe, there to carry on his life-long work; Norton, the lecturer upon art, future editor of Carlyle's letters; Cabot, a veteran contributor to the *Dial;* Whipple, with two-storied head and bulbous spectacles, keen critic and good talker. There were frequently other writers less known to fame. Of those mentioned, Holmes, Dwight, Cabot, and Norton alone survive.

But one constant visitor is not to be overlooked. This was —

> "The Jedge that covers with his hat
> More wit an' gumption, an' shrewd Yankee sense
> Than there is mosses on an ol' stone fence."

"The Jedge"[1] was not a contributor; he called himself *amicus curiæ.* His ready wit, solid ability, and social graces made him one of the delights of all literary gatherings. He was leaving the table quite early one day, when M. Fontarive, who had

[1] Hon. E. Rockwood Hoar.

served a fine *menu*, appeared with a bowl
of flaming punch that diffused "Sabæan
odors." Still "The Jedge" edged toward
the door, excusing himself by saying that
he had befqre him a long journey in the
train. "Stay," said the Autocrat, "and
take some punch; 'twill shorten the distance." — "Yes," replied "The Jedge,"
"and double the prospect." He was as
full of stories as Lord Cockburn, and rarely
left the table without flinging some *mot*
as a souvenir. "The Jedge" survives:
late be his departure for the last train.
George T. Davis, a wonderful *raconteur*,
sometimes came, and the guests remained
for hours to hear him. It is said that
Abraham Lincoln once sat with him till
morning, and declared he was the best
story-teller he had ever met. John C. Wyman (one of the firm of publishers) was
also a wonderful artist in touching up a
story, as well as a brilliant talker. His
imitations, as of Webster's grand manner,
were perfect, and often astounding. He is
still fresh and vivacious, while Davis has
"gone over to the majority."

There was no lack of serious and even
spiritual conversation. Holmes's fire often
fused reasoning into eloquence; and his

sentences had such force, proportion, and finish that they would not have needed revision for print. Lowell always talked well, and often brilliantly. He *soared* naturally, as if the high regions of imagination were his familiar haunts. And the hearer never felt that Lowell had done his best; for there was something like a restrained intensity, which gave the impression that he was always greater than anything he had done. Every competent observer felt sure that his career would be a *crescendo*.

Emerson was fond of listening, but after a set-to he often made a philosophic summary or *scholium* that was beautiful and memorable. One day Dr. Holmes was speaking casually of architecture, and observed that all the orders might, roughly speaking, be resolved into three,— the Egyptian, characterized by breadth of base; the Grecian, in which there was an agreeable proportion between base and height; and the Gothic, in which the height was extreme. Mr. Emerson sat with eyes far away, and said in his deep, level tone, as if merely communing with himself, "That furnishes a striking analogy. The broad-based Egyptian was for the repose of the dead; the harmonious Grecian was for the activities and pleasures of the living, and the aspiring lines of the Gothic, do they not lead our thoughts toward immortality? "

Volumes could have been made of the bright discussions which were lost in air. But they were not wholly lost, for they left their impression in the minds of survivors, and so have been disseminated.

On one occasion the women contributors were invited. Several were expected, but only two came, Mrs. Harriet Beecher Stowe, and Mrs. Harriet Prescott Spofford. Mrs. Stowe had demurred at first, and only consented upon the stipulation that there should be no wine on the table. Cigars were, of course, out of the question. The condition was agreed to, for all were desirous of doing honor to the woman who had taken such a distinguished part in the great question of the day. The dinner passed agreeably, though the ladies did not have a great deal to say. Crystal jars and pitchers of iced water were plentiful along the table, and if by chance a few of them had a judicious mingling of some other pale beverage, the pervading scent of flowers that filled the room would have smothered the guilty secret. The sparkle of surprise in some faces when the glasses were raised was as good as a play.

In all that belonged to these dinners there was, no doubt, a certain provincial note which was a great part of the charm. In a small city, such as Boston then was, there was leisure and chance for intimacy, and the relations of men, and especially of authors, were on an easy footing rarely attainable in a metropolis, where life is a struggle and the literary guild is rent with factions and jealousies. In Scott's Diary (March 7, 1827), after jotting down his impressions of a gathering in Edinburgh, he says, "Can London give such a dinner? It may, but I never saw one. They are too cold and critical to be so easily pleased." The reader who is acquainted with our literature, and has followed the course of the *Atlantic*, knows that in this sketch there is only the design to show some of the eminent early contributors. An account of that magazine would include a great many brilliant writers whose fame at the beginning was not so conspicuous. Prominent among these are Col. T. W. Higginson, John T. Trowbridge, and Rose Terry Cooke. Prescott wrote, but he was in delicate health, and (in his mature years at least) was not clubable.

During the first two years Lowell wrote a number of political articles, a few poems, and a great many book-notices. His contributions were more interesting and of greater force after 1862, when he was free from the duties of editor.

At the beginning the editor's salary was three thousand dollars, — receiving also pay for his contributions like the others. The usual rates for the best writers were ten dollars a page for prose, and an average of fifty dollars for a poem. The *Atlantic* was not able to pay the prices given to leading authors to-day. But Lowell and the fraternity were fully satisfied.

VI.

In 1857, not far from the time when the *Atlantic* was started, Lowell was married to Miss Frances Dunlap of Portland, Me. The ceremony was performed according to the rite of the Episcopal Church by his brother Robert. Miss Dunlap belonged to a good family, and was possessed of a fine mind and quiet force of character. She was a most attractive woman without being remarkably beautiful. Her profile was Greek, her hair luxuriant, and her calm eyes sweetly expressive. She had been well taught, and, for some time previous to the marriage, had had charge of the education of Lowell's daughter, his only living child. She gained the respect and affection of all Lowell's relatives and friends. Simplicity, dignity, and grace were charmingly blended in her manners.

After his marriage Lowell went to live with Dr. Estes Howe in a house near the college grounds. Dr. Howe's wife was a sister of Maria White Lowell. He was greatly esteemed, and by his intimates heartily loved. He was a member of the whist-club, and a guest at all the literary dinners. The affection between him and Lowell was tender and constant. After a time Lowell went back to Elmwood to live. He was most happy in his marriage, as his wife shared his tastes, and was a woman · to be loved.

He had never been a steady worker, which is not remarkable in a poet; beyond that, he was dilatory and procrastinating to such a degree that, without some (carefully concealed) encouragement, he might have gone on indefinitely,—

"Involved in a paulo-post-future of song."

His wife was surely his good angel, and the results of his labors after his second marriage show that he had been animated by new resolution. In writing a poem like "The Cathedral," there was great strain upon his vital forces; and when such a work was in progress her unobstrusive ministrations were soothing and sustaining.

She died in London while her husband was minister. No children were born of the marriage.

Before commenting upon the second series of "Biglow Papers," it may be of service to make a brief statement for the benefit of younger readers; for it must be remembered that a generation has grown up since the Civil War. There were two distinct classes of anti-slavery men. Lowell began with one, and afterward acted with the other. One was the party of Garrison and Phillips, known as abolitionists, which relied solely upon moral influences. The other brought the question into politics, endeavoring to restrain slavery by law, to prevent its spreading into free territory, and to make it the strictly limited exception, instead of the masterful and aggressive rule, in the republic. This was called at first the Liberty Party, then the Free-Soil Party, and was always a minor third as against the Whigs and Democrats, until, in the campaign for the election of Lincoln in 1860, it was consolidated with the former under the name of Republican. The Wilmot Proviso (proposed by David Wilmot, M.C., of Pennsylvania) had been the prominent issue for a number of years. It was designed to exclude slavery from the Territories, which previous to becoming States are under the control of Congress.

The cry of the Free-Soilers, was " Freedom national, slavery sectional." The Proviso was staved off, could not be made law; but what was done proved effectual in the end,—namely, each Territory when about to become a State was allowed to choose between freedom and slavery. Then ensued a race for the occupation of the coming new States such as the world had never seen. The party of freedom won Kansas and Nebraska by superior activity, organization, and resources, but not without long and violent contests with murderous "border ruffians," the partisans of slavery from the adjacent State of Missouri. Some of the most thrilling incidents in American history are to be found in the record of this life-and-death struggle, in which John Brown of Ossawatomie played a leading part.

A passage in the second series (No. Two) refers to this glorious result : —

"O strange New World, that yit wast never young,
  Whose youth from thee by gripin' need was wrung,

    *   *   *   *   *   *   *   *

An' who grew'st strong thru shifts an' wants an'
  pains,
Nussed by stern men with empires in their brains,

    *   *   *   *   *   *   *   *

Thou, skilled by Freedom an' by gret events,
To pitch new states ez Old World men pitch tents,
 * * * * * * * *
The grave's not dug where traitor hands shall lay
In fearful haste thy murdered corse away.''

Some of these lines may challenge comparison with the most vigorous in the
language.

After this crushing defeat came the election of Abraham Lincoln; and then the
leaders in the slave-holding States, seeing
that all was lost, brought about secession
from the Union, and took up arms for a
Southern Confederacy.

Before long Lowell bethought him of the
characters and stage properties of his old
comedy, and brought out from retirement
Hosea Biglow, *Parson Wilbur*, and *Birdo-
fredum Sawin* to figure in a new drama;
deepest of tragedies it proved to be for
him. The scampish volunteer of the Mexican War had become a slaveholder and
secessionist, and furnished what matter for
satire he might; while *Hosea* was the mouth-
piece of moral convictions, of patriotic fer-
vor, and of faith in the indestructible unity
of a free nation,—a unity not too dearly
bought, even with the blood of the best and
dearest. The Mexican War, though dis-

graceful, was waged on foreign soil, and, in modern view, a small affair. The War of the Rebellion was an ever-present and tremendous fact, and while it lasted there was no room, within or without, for anything else. The new series is wholly occupied with matters connected with the war, and naturally wants much of the comic relief of its predecessor; but it is an error to think it inferior as poetry. Probably the most forcible part is that in which the poet deals with the course of Great Britain in favoring the Rebellion, — the dialogue between Concord Bridge and Bunker's Hill Monument, — followed by the regretful, manly, and ringing reproaches in "Jonathan to John." The prefatory letter of *Parson Wilbur* is, in its way, a more effective statement of the case of the seizure of Mason and Slidell than any made by Secretary Seward.

Two other poems of the series (Nos. six and ten) should be mentioned, because they are at Lowell's high-water mark, and cannot be easily paralleled in verse of our time. "Sunthin' in the Pastoral Line" contains pictures of spring in the country which in completeness, felicity, and vividness excel all his descriptions in serious verse. It is

an almanac of blossoms and bird-notes,
with scarcely a blank page left for a contin-
uator. *Hosea's* interview with a Puritan
ancestor, which forms the sequel, is in the
poet's most vigorous manner.   He truly
says of the Yankee dialect, —

> "For puttin' in a downright lick
> 'Twixt Humbug's eyes there's few can metch it,
> An' then it *helves* my thought ez slick
> Ez stret-grained hickory doos a hetchet."

"A Letter to the Editor of the *Atlantic
Monthly*" (No. ten) is a poem of which no
description can give an adequate notion.
It winds its way with an apparent artless-
ness; with hints of tender and half-humor-
ous thought; with glimpses of rural scenes,
and of "farm-smokes, sweetest sight on
airth;" and with a melancholy sense of the
merciless obsession of the war.   Then it
breaks into an agony of lament for the
young heroes fallen in battle, and closes
with an apostrophe to Peace which few who
are old enough to remember those terrible
days can read, even for the twentieth time,
with dry eyes.   It is not Peace coming "as
a mourner bowed" that is invoked, but
Peace —

> "with hand on hilt,
> And step that proves her Victory's daughter."

The reader seems to have slowly ascended a hill like Pisgah, and is facing a prospect that awes him to silence. No description can convey this eloquence of the heart. It rouses emotions, at least in those who knew the awful war, which we must call sublime.

Mention was made of his nephew Putnam. Another, Lieutenant James Jackson Lowell, was killed at Seven Pines; the third, General Charles Russell Lowell, at Winchester. The last-named was wounded while leading a charge of cavalry; and, though he knew the wound was mortal. he was helped upon his horse, and headed another brilliant charge, in which he was again hit, and died the next day. It is this heroic act, never surpassed, which is referred to in the lines following. They are often repeated at the reunions of the veterans of the war.

> " Rat-tat-tat-tattle thru the street
>   I hear the drummers makin' riot,
>   An' I set thinkin' o' the feet
>   Thet follered once, an' now are quiet, —
>   White feet, ez snowdrops innercent,
>   That never knowed the paths o' Sat'n,
>   Whose comin' step ther's ears thet won't,
>   No, not lifelong, leave off awaitin'.

Why, haint I held 'em on my knee?
  Didn't I love to see 'em growin',
Three likely lads ez wal could be,
  Hahnsome an' brave, an' not tu knowin'?
I set an' look into the blaze,
  Whose natur', jes like theirn, keeps climbin',
Ez long 'z it lives, in shinin' ways,
  An' half despise myself for rhymin'.

Wut's words tu them whose faith an' truth
  On War's red techstone rang true metal,
Who ventered life an' love an' youth
  For the gret prize o' death in battle? —
To him — who, deadly hurt, agen
  Flashed on afore the charge's thunder,
Tippin' with fire the bolt of men
  Thet rived the Rebel line asunder? "

For nearly ten years (1863–1872) Lowell, in collaboration with Charles Eliot
Norton, was editor of the *North American
Review*, in which many of his essays appeared. This was a scholarly and sedate
periodical, whose history began with the be-
ginnings of our literature. It was read and
respected by cultivated people, but made
no appeal to the general public by means
of sensational articles or vaunted names.
Its subscribers and friends appreciated
thorough and finished essays, such as
Lowell's and Norton's, — essays of which a
larger public, a public of a hundred thousand, would be easily tired.

The "Commemoration Ode" (1865), considered by many as the best of the poems
called out by the war, made a powerful
impression. Some readers, perhaps, need
to be informed that there was a proposal
to erect a Memorial Hall in honor of the
sons of Harvard who fell in the Civil War,
and that the Ode was read at a gathering
of the friends of the university. The noble
hall, with Norman tower, which has since
arisen, and which forms such a landmark,
needs only the mellowing touch of age to
become one of the most impressive of col-
legiate buildings. The Ode was recited
in a broad tent set up near the college
grounds, following an address by General
Meade, the hero of Gettysburg. Lowell
usually appeared composed, if not cold, in
public; but on this occasion his voice and
manner showed that the scene and the subject had wholly possessed him. The *white*
illumination of his features, as he warmed
to the impassioned close of the poem, was
like a transfiguration. The effect upon the
great assembly of people, who, with flushed,
or eager, or tearful faces, followed every
line with breathless attention, was something never to be forgotten. The memories
of the war then were like half-healed
wounds.

MR. LOWELL IN LATER MIDDLE LIFE.

VII.

"UNDER The Willows," published in 1869, and dedicated to Norton, contains the best work of the poet's maturer years, together with some lighter pieces of an earlier date. The title comes from a group of large spreading trees on the bank of Charles River, a favorite resort of students. With few exceptions these poems presuppose too much in ordinary readers to be widely popular. This is not the case with "The First Snow Fall," which, like "The Changeling" and "She Came and Went," in a former volume, is as simple and touching as a white stone for a child's grave. Equally open to view is the theme of "The Dead House." But in many of the pieces in this volume the thought is subtile and remote; and ordinary readers, if candid, would confess that they "did not know what it was all about." Lowell's mind was fertile in recondite as well as in obvious allusion, and he had long dealt with abstruse ideas; so that he never reflected that

even fairly well-read people might need a
clew to his meaning.   He was never wil-
fully obscure, like Browning, but his
thought is often to be sought for.

Like every collection of true poetry, this
book is a gathering of the memories and
fancies of years; each one an ideal *replica*
of some experience or mood.   Thus, "Gold
Egg" is a reminiscence of German University life, a misty blending of metaphysics,
mythology, and the "Arabian Nights," —
dissimilarities *conjured* into a strange harmony by the magic of genius.   "A Winter
Evening Hymn to My Fire," written almost
forty years ago, is a fantasy in verse of free
movement, and is itself as airy as flame.
The devotee of tobacco will smile at the
classic pedigree of the goddess Nicotia, and
will regale himself with the picture of
smoke that —

> "floats and curls
> In airy spires and wayward whirls,
> Or poises on its tremulous stalk
> A flower of frailest revery."

The poem, "To John Bartlett, On His
Sending Me a Seven-Pound Trout," is an
example of Lowell's playful and delicate
art.   The first eager joy over the size and
beauty of the fish is Rabelaisian.   Then we

see the fisherman threading his way through the woodland mysteries; then the rise, the struggle, and the capture, — all as vivid as if the scenes were before our eyes. The grotesque rhymes are among the most curious in Lowell's vocabulary.

In other poems are sketches of sea-beaten Appledore, of the marshy banks of Charles River, or of lusty boyhood in the Cambridge of the old time. Perhaps the subtilest power of expression is seen in " The Foot Path," a purely ideal or transcendental poem, which leads from solid earth, the reader scarcely perceives how or when, into the realm of the infinite.

THE FOOT PATH.

It mounts athwart the windy hill
    Through sallow slopes of upland bare,
And Fancy climbs with foot-fall still
    Its narrowing curves that end in air.

By day a warmer-hearted blue
    Stoops softly to that topmost swell;
Its thread-like windings seem a clew
    To gracious climes where all is well.

By night, far yonder, I surmise
    An ampler world than clips my ken,
Where the great stars of happier skies
    Commingle nobler fates of men.

I look and long, then haste me home,
  Still master of my secret rare;
Once tried, the path would end in Rome,
  But now it leads me everywhere,

Forever to the new it guides
  From former good, old overmuch;
What Nature for her poets hides
  'Tis wiser to divine than clutch.

The bird I list hath never come
  Within the scope of mortal ear;
My prying step would make him dumb,
  And the fair tree, his shelter, sear.

Behind the hill, behind the sky,
  Behind my inmost thought, he sings;
No feet avail; to hear it nigh
  The song itself must lend the wings.

Sing on, sweet bird, close hid, and raise
  Those angel stairways in my brain,
That climb from these low-vaulted days
  To spacious sunshines far from pain.

Sing when thou wilt, enchantment fleet,
  I leave thy covert haunt untrod,
And envy Science not her feat
  To make a twice-told tale of God.

They said the fairies tript no more,
  And long ago that Pan was dead;
'Twas but that fools preferred to bore
  Earth's rind inch-deep for truth instead.

Pan leaps and pipes all summer long,
  The fairies dance each full-mooned night,
Would we but doff our lenses strong,
  And trust our wiser eyes' delight.

City of Elf-land, just without
  Our seeing, marvel ever new,
Glimpsed in fair weather, a sweet doubt
  Sketched-in, mirage-like on the blue.

I build thee in yon sunset cloud,
  Whose edge allures to climb the height,
I hear thy drowned bells inly-loud,
  From still pools dusk with dreams of night.

Thy gates are shut to hardiest will,
  Thy countersign of long-lost speech, —
Those fountained courts, those chambers still
  Fronting Time's far East, who shall reach?

I know not and will never pry,
  But trust our human heart for all;
Wonders that from the seeker fly
  Into an open sense may fall.

Hide in thine own soul, and surprise
  The password of the unwary elves;
Seek it, thou canst not bribe their spies;
  Unsought, they whisper it themselves.

"The Washers of the Shroud," written
in a high prophetic strain, recalls the awful suspense in an early crisis in the Civil
War. "Villa Franca" shows the Fates

dooming for his crimes Napoleon III.; and
it was written years before the fall of Se-
dan. Powerful poems these last; and some
years later they were referred to by Lowell,
in conversation with the writer, with just
pride in the intuitive foresight shown. But
it should be said that he seldom spoke of
his own works, even to friends, and almost
never read to them a poem.

While Lowell and a few other American
poets have inclined to choose spiritual
themes, the British poets have generally
looked for subjects in common life, and
dealt with the strong and enduring feelings, — with what is most vital in the nature
of man. For this reason they have taken
the stronger hold upon mankind. Landor
says, "The human heart is the world of
poetry; the imagination is only its atmosphere." This is one reason why, since
the prevalence of the transcendental mood
here, poems like "Enoch Arden" and
"Dora" have seldom been conceived. On
the other hand, those who shun idealism
will be in danger of falling into a real-
ism which paralyzes and blights the finer
sensibilities. The sturdy realist, without
spiritual intuitions, will read with unblest

eyes not only the most exalted of Lowell's poems, but the essays and poems of Emerson, and many of the most beautiful of the tales of Hawthorne.

Tennyson was both realist and idealist; and with his death most of the poetry of the Victorian era came to an end. Meredith and Swinburne sustain the traditions.

It may be well to mention here that in our poetry descriptions of landscape have occupied relatively a large space. Instances are everywhere visible. T. Buchanan Read put all his power into "The Closing Scene," a magnificent autumn picture which is likely to endure. Bryant was almost exclusively a landscape artist. Whittier was profuse with the pictures which serve as introductions to many of his poems. He and Lowell were the two conspicuously faithful of our scenery painters,—giving not merely picturesque outlooks, but exact details, as in a Dutch masterpiece. This is not to decry their art, but to indicate their method by pointing to the delicacy of the strokes. Longfellow loved landscapes, and painted them well; but in his treatment there was only general truth, without pretence of nicety of detail.

Leaving one side purely scenic poems, which have a recognized but minor place, the truth appears to be that natural objects are important only as accessories: they are to support and set off the great picture; air and clouds are to give softness, depth and distance; while imagination casts its spell in high lights and glooms; but the centre and soul is in the human interest, — in the visible play of contending emotions, in the spectacle of heroic patience, of noble ambition, or of fortitude superior to fate.

This is not wandering from Lowell's poetry. It has, as we have seen, many phases, and its place in the future appears assured. But a subtile idealism, and a passion for elaborate landscape painting, though both qualities imply a high order of genius, do not take a firm hold upon the great world of readers. The exquisite ideal conceptions, and the marvellous execution of poems "in the pastoral line," are for the few; while poems in which the thought is less fine-spun, and which glow with emotion, or show the workings of the human heart, impress all who have any love for poetry.

"The Cathedral," which was published a year later, is equally beyond the compre-

hension of ordinary readers. In fact, there
is no way to communicate the central ideas
of the poem to any but trained minds. The
story, which is of a visit to Chartres, is
slight; the burden of the poem appears to
be a meditation upon the Divine government, and its relations with man, — leading
to an idealist's indignant protest against
the drift of a materialistic age. Or it may
be looked upon as the philosophy of religion in its relations with art and science in
human life; and this is presented from
what may be called the mediæval view. Yet
it is far enough from discussion, which de-
poetizes; and from dogmatism, which pet-
rifies. There are many gleaming points in
the descriptions, but the strongest impression is made by the suggestions of faith and
repose, which, like the glimpses of beauty
in the gray stones of the building, touch
the heart through the imagination.

The vocabulary for such a poem must be
ample; no sweet simplicity is possible for
him who would frame metaphysical conceptions in verse, or reproduce the glan-
cing lights which an aging poet sees playing
over old shrines and old beliefs. The tone
is indicative of a reaction, as in the case
of Tennyson; painful at first to those who

once felt their pulses thrilled in reading
"The Present Crisis" of the one, and the
"Locksley Hall" of the other.

"The Cathedral" is a poem to be medi-
tated upon, or, if the vulgarism may be par-
doned, *chewed over.* It gives an earnest
reader strange sensations. Like the edifice
it treats of, it is incrusted with precious
imagery, and it towers with sky-reaching
thought.

In 1870 were published two volumes of
collected essays: "My Study Windows"
and "Among My Books." A second volume with the latter title came out in 1876.

In 1872 he went to Europe, and did not
return until 1874. He received honors
from the universities of Oxford and Cambridge, and was welcomed everywhere by
men of letters. Just before he went abroad
there appeared a series of labored articles
upon his prose works, arguing that they
could not become classic on account of
their vicious style. The ground had been
laid out like a siege by Turenne, and it
was intended, evidently, that the offending
essayist should have what is called "a
good setting down."* To a friend who vol-
unteered to write a reply Lowell sent a
note, a part of which is here given, mainly

for the sake of the six lines of verse not elsewhere printed.

ELMWOOD, 12th May, 1871.

. . . " Don't bother yourself with any sympathy for me under my supposed sufferings from critics. I don't need it in the least. If a man does anything good, the world always finds it out sooner or later; and, if he doesn't, the world finds *that* out too — and ought.

> "'Gainst monkey's claw and ass's hoof
> My studies forge me mail of proof:
> I climb through paths forever new
> To purer air and broader view.
> What matter though they should efface,
> So far below, my footstep's trace!'"

He was resolute all his life to make no reply to criticism of his works or of his politics.

The death of Agassiz, which occurred in 1874, was the subject of a poem which is much more than a personal tribute. It is of considerable length, varied in its themes, dignified in movement, and forms a monument which will outlast brass and marble. Besides the reminiscences of loving intimacy, the work shows a poet's power in lines of description which burn into the memory, and a poet's mastery of sustained philosophic thought. The great Helvetian stands before us as in life. No one ever saw him but had a vivid impression of virile and engaging personality. The noble head, well placed on expansive shoulders, and the look of mingled sagacity, energy, and good-humor were never forgotten. Whoever remembers him thinks first of his smile.

In one place Lowell shows him at a literary dinner: —

> " The mass Teutonic toned to Gallic grace,
> The eyes where sunshine runs before the lips,
> While Holmes's rockets curve their long ellipse,
> And burst in seeds of fire that burst again,
> To drop in scintillating rain."

He shows us Emerson, —

> "the face half rustic, half divine,
> Self-poised, sagacious, streaked with humor fine,"

and he curiously notes —

> "—the wise nose's firm-built aquiline."

The study of Hawthorne's rather melancholy face is extremely subtle: —

> "November nature with a name of May."

There is a brief sketch of Longfellow, one of Felton, and one of Arthur Hugh

Clough, the English poet who lived for a year near Elmwood, and afterwards died at Florence.

Some of the brooding thoughts touch the heart as the eyes follow the lines: —

" ' Tis lips long cold that give the warmest kiss,
' Tis the lost voice comes oftenest to our ears,
We count our rosary by the beads we miss."

Only a great mind could have conceived this many-branched poem; only a generous heart could have so permeated it with love and sorrow; only a poet could have sustained its thought and feeling in such stately and impressive lines. Few of Lowell's poems better show his native qualities, and the art of which he was master.

The tribute is to be found in "Heartsease and Rue," the volume which was published while he was minister to Great Britain.

Three noble odes were written at the time of the United States Centennial Celebrations: one read at Concord, April 19, 1875; one read at Cambridge, July 3, 1876, being mainly a tribute to Washington and the State of Virginia; the third for the Fourth of July, 1876. They have great lifts of imagination and billows of passion, and, with "The Commemoration Ode," rank among the poet's best works. The Three Odes are dedicated to E. L. Godkin, editor of the *Nation*.

VIII.

WE saw Lowell as a youth, a writer of rather frivolous verse; then a lover inditing sonnets; then a reformer with the earnestness and high purpose of a primitive Christian; then a satirist and a delineator of Yankee character, to serve a great cause; then a patriot, devoted to the unity and glory of country; and then a philosophic poet reasoning upon the dealings of the Almighty with men, and meditating upon duty and destiny, — faith and the immortal life. His literary career was a steady upward movement.

He had never held office,[1] not even that of justice of the peace, a very common and common-place honor in Massachusetts. At the age of fifty-eight he began public life at the top. The traditions of the government had favored the appointment of literary men to diplomatic and consular posts. The

[1] He was a member of the Republican Convention which nominated Hayes for President, and was also chosen presidential elector, — an office which, by force of circumstances, has become purely honorary and without any serious duty.

names of Irving, Bancroft, Marsh, Hawthorne, Motley, Bayard Taylor, and Bret
Harte readily come to mind. President
Hayes, at the suggestion, it is said, of
Howells, the novelist, offered to Lowell
the Austrian mission, which he declined.
Motley had found life in Vienna uninter-
esting. Whatever Lowell's reason for de-
clining may have been, he subsequently
accepted the appointment to Spain, possibly because he was then engaged in the
study of Cervantes and the Spanish drama.
In due time, upon the retirement of Minister Welch, he was transferred from Madrid
to London. He was then sixty years old.
His youth, with its enthusiasm, its hopes
and deceptions, was far behind. His fame
rose full-orbed upon Great Britain, and
he had a reception seldom given to a
stranger. He was again made welcome
by men eminent in letters and in social
rank, and was especially honored by the
Queen. The islands seemed brighter for
his coming, and fresh ties of sympathy and
respect seemed to unite the elder and the
younger peoples. How he bore himself in
this place, the place of the highest dignity
in the gift of the President, is fresh in the
minds of all. He was a lover of his country,

jealous of its honor, a patriot in every fibre; while at the same time he was a citizen of the world of letters, and loved history in minsters and castles, and was conservative of the poetry of tradition. No one was more firmly based in the common language, or better read in the common literature, of our race. Englishmen knew he was the unchanged author of " Jonathan to John;" and if he retained his popularity, as he undoubtedly did, it was not by cringing, or surrender of democratic ideas, or suppression of unpalatable truth. It is in the blood of our race to admire a manly man.

His numerous addresses throughout the kingdom gave evidence of his mature thought, scholarship, and grand style: they testify to the honor and respect in which he was held. A selection from these was published, entitled, " Democracy and Other Addresses."

With the coming in of President Cleveland in 1885, Lowell knew that by a rule in the Department of State he would be superseded. He had had enough of public life, and did not desire to remain in office; and he welcomed his successor Mr. Phelps with cordiality. He told the writer that he recognized the ability and training of that gentleman as quite superior to his own; that his (Lowell's) legal acquirements were slight and becoming obsolete, and, moreover, had never included constitutional or international law; while Mr. Phelps was an eminent jurist, versed in history and able to take up any question in diplomacy with mastery. Upon this topic he spoke with earnestness and at some length. He said he had been treated with proper consideration, and had nothing but good-will and high regard for President Cleveland. At a dinner in Boston after his return he spoke in a similar strain of the President, to the disgust of those who think it treason to party to admit any excellence in an opponent. But Lowell was never a thick-and-thin politician, and still less a political trimmer. He had independent views on national questions, and, in regard to men, his just and unprejudiced mind recognized good qualities by whomsoever manifested.

In 1888 was published a collection of poems entitled "Heartsease and Rue." They were mostly productions of later years, but one of them was "Fitz Adam's Story," written long before as the first of a series of Chaucerian tales, never to be completed.

For some years he spent his summers in London and his winters in Boston, or with his daughter, Mrs. Edward Burnett, in Southboro, Mass. When her two sons were about to enter Harvard College the family removed to Elmwood, and the poet went to live with them. He had long shrunk from returning there, as the house was "full of ghosts," he said. There had died his mother and father, his sister Rebecca, his first wife, and three or four infants. From the upper windows westward there is a lookout over the cemetery of Mount Auburn, where these loved ones rest. There at length he was settled, planning another visit to London for the following summer, — a visit never to be made.

He had an inherited tendency to gout, and suffered at times severely. Even as far back as 1857 there were times when the pain seized the soles of his feet so sharply that he would lift them spasmodically high in air, with half-suppressed groans that were heartaching to hear. Still, his health was ordinarily good, and his body, though never robust, seemed equal to the demands of a life that was generally kept within simple limits. It was seldom that any illness sent him to his bed. In 1885, when he was leaving office in London, he seemed to have visibly aged; his shoulders were getting bowed, his face was thinner, his forehead more deeply lined and corrugated, and his hair and beard growing gray. Still, as he had always been active, temperate, and extremely careful of his health, his friends looked forward to see him reach fourscore. It was impossible to think of the creator of *Hosea Biglow* as growing old. But in the latter part of 1890 disquieting reports came from Elmwood: disease had attacked a vital organ, and the worst was feared. Time passed without real amendment, and in August, 1891, after long and terrible suffering, he found relief in death.

By his desire the funeral services were performed at the College Chapel by clergymen of the Episcopal Church. The two surviving members of the whist-club then living in Cambridge were among the pallbearers. His death produced a deep impression, and the newspapers were full of tributes from writers of every class. Those who best knew him mourned his loss with a sorrow that was to end only with life.

IX.

THE time has not come for an impartial estimate of Lowell's works; — not for those who lived within the sphere of his influence; still less for those who felt the undying affection which his manly and generous qualities inspired. In some respects his works appeal more strongly to his country-men than to sympathetic readers in Great Britain. For a Briton cannot enter into his passionate devotion to the American Union, nor become enraptured over his prophecies of this country's future glory. Patriotic poems are for home-consumption, as are the brutally frank petitions to God in national hymns, such as: —

> "Confound their politics,
> Frustrate their knavish tricks,
> On us Thy blessing fix," etc.

But there were other patriotic features in Lowell's poetry. Setting aside foreign "larks and daisies," and all conventional-ity, he set himself to sing of the birds and flowers he knew, the landscapes and the men he had seen, the speech he had heard, and the unborrowed feelings of his own soul. His verse, therefore, excepting that of his earliest years, is no echo of English poetry, although he was master of its manifold vocabulary. In respect to his truth to nature, he is the most American of poets, unless it may be Whittier ; and his faithfulness is a stumbling-block to English readers. How is a Briton to conceive of the multitude of bright objects peculiar to the New World which are sketched in Lowell's verse? The difficulties in rustic speech and manners are well nigh insurmountable: however popular the " Biglow Papers " may be in Great Britain, not one reader there in a thousand really comprehends the talk of *Hosea*, or the rustic charm of "The Courtin'," any more than he comprehends the poems of Burns.

In the United States, though the comedy and satire of Lowell were immediately recognized, his serious poems were appreciated by few until long after they were published. Setting aside the inveterate party prejudice which cast a cloud over all he wrote, there was something in his verse which left common readers in bewilderment

or indifference. It was a new combination
of elements, and it was distasteful to all
whose souls had not been "touched to finer
issues." No complete analysis can be
given, but we may observe these : —

First, Truth towards God, his fellow-
men, the world of nature, and himself.
Second, Idealism, including eternity of being, the immanence of God in the soul,
the supremacy of right, and the aspiration
to a spiritual existence, including a spiritual conception of this present life. Third,
Brotherhood, in the sense taught by Christ,
and ignored in most Christian pulpits.
Fourth, Beauty, for its own sake, but
always arm in arm with Strength, both
ministering to mortal and immortal needs.
Fifth, Melody, when compatible with other
indispensable qualities.

It was an unattractive combination to the
American readers of poetry forty years ago.

Men professedly seek for originality,
and at the same time demand finish and
grace; not perceiving that grace and originality are almost always at variance, and
tend to exclude each other. Grace is
the thing accepted, accustomed, expected;
originality is startling, reactionary, and
gives us pause.

A poet with such a genius for veracity could never be conventional: he must write from fresh feelings and impressions. He could not be led by fashions in art, or philosophy, or politics. He could not pass by the poor and the outcast at his own door,— it was easy to pass by the leprous beggar of eighteen hundred years ago. He cared little for poetry which was not uplifting to the soul, or useful to humanity.

So we see that his ideal notions of right, truth, brotherhood, and spiritual life are the animating soul of the greater number of his serious poems. Reference has been made to the splendor and power of "The Present Crisis," and others of that early period. It is interesting, also, to notice how he has employed the old legends to inculcate charity, tolerance, and Christian love. Listen to the blessed resolution of the discord in the final harmony of Godminster chimes! Look at the beautiful parable of the cups of differing size in the symbolic dream of Ambrose! Admire the secret of integrity and fortitude carried in Dara's great soul, and in his empty campchest! Think of the persistence of conscience in the pathetic story of Rhœcus! As for Sir Launfal, it is picture, legend, and Christian parable in one. Such poems need no added "application;" they are themselves their own moral. Even in a personal poem, like "The Dandelion," there is something in the boyish memories to remind us that —

" Heaven lies about us in our infancy."

It is interesting to look at resemblances, so as to speculate upon the influences that may have affected a poet's style. Every artist begins by imitation, and happy is he who emerges betimes from control, and establishes his own individuality. At the beginning there were some suggestions of Tennyson's early manner, — a certain daintiness, and the use of obsolescent words. This did not remain, for the nature of Lowell was virile and robust. We can see that he was one with Chaucer in his joy in nature, and in the intuitive perception of character. He is moved by the frank flow of Dryden's lusty song; by the quaintness of Donne, and the directness and energy of Marvell, in the green shade of whose mystical Garden both Emerson and Lowell might have lingered.

"Beaver Brook" may perhaps furnish an illustration of Lowell's poetical method, —

if a sure instinct ever makes use of a method,
— and show the shining qualities and the
infelicities of his verse.   Let us suppose
that an ordinary man, a Philistine, — if
readers prefer that name, — had walked by
that little brook on a summer afternoon,
at a time before the mill had become a
ruin.   He saw, as he passed, a sunlit valley
lying below a hill on whose slope fell the
shadow of a cedar.   In the open door of
the mill stood a whitened miller; but, as all
millers are floury, this one called for no
special remark.   The great wheel was
turning under a slender stream of water
coming from a reservoir formed by dam-
ming the brook.   He did not see Undine,
or Kühleborn, or any of their tribe, tripping
over the wheel: he saw only the splashing
water, and heard only the din of the whirl-
ing mill-stones; and with a listless glance
he passed on.   Now, keeping in mind the
literal description that would be given by
the man without a poet's vision, let us see
what the poem shows us: —

BEAVER BROOK.

Hushed with broad sunlight lies the hill,
And, minuting the long day's loss,
The cedar's shadow, slow and still,
Creeps o'er its dial of gray moss.

Warm noon brims full the valley's cup,
  The aspen's leaves are scarce astir;
Only the little mill sends up
  Its busy, never-ceasing burr.

Climbing the loose-piled wall that hems
  The road along the mill-pond's brink,
From 'neath the arching barberry stems
  My footstep scares the shy chewink.

Beneath a bony buttonwood
  The mill's red door lets forth the din;
The whitened miller, dust-imbued,
  Flits past the square of dark within.

No mountain torrent's strength is here;
  Sweet Beaver, child of forest still,
Heaps its small pitcher to the ear,
  And gently waits the miller's will.

Swift slips Undine along the race
  Unheard, and then with flashing bound
Floods the dull wheel with light and grace,
  And, laughing, hunts the loath drudge round.

The miller dreams not at what cost
  The quivering mill-stones hum and whirl,
Nor how for every turn are tost
  Armfuls of diamond and of pearl.

But summer cleared my happier eyes
  With drops of some celestial juice,
To see how Beauty underlies
  Forevermore each form of use.

And more; methought I saw that flood,
  Which now so dull and darkling steals,
Thick, here and there, with human blood,
  To turn the world's laborious wheels.

No more than doth the miller there,
  Shut in our several cells, do we
Know with what waste of beauty rare
  Moves every day's machinery.

Surely the wiser time shall come,
  When this fine overplus of might,
No longer sullen, slow, and dumb,
  Shall leap to music and to light.

In that new childhood of the Earth
  Life of itself shall dance and play,
Fresh blood in Time's shrunk veins make mirth,
  And labor meet delight half-way.

The landscape is a picture of harmonious details. The brook is spiritualized, and sets machinery going in the brain as well as in the mill. While we are thinking of the crystal gleam of the falling water, we are suddenly appalled at the blood which "turns the world's laborious wheels." And, as we come to the inspiring hope of the "wiser time," we are about to say that that poem fulfils all high conditions, when suddenly we are forced to stop. We stop, because we remember the melodists. What

will they say of *"Swift slips* Undine " — or
of "child of *forest still" ?* What will they
say of this line, —

" And, laughing, hunts the loath drudge round " ?

See how the consonants stand out like
tense muscles on a gymnast's arm! Or,
look at this row of jolting monosyllables : —

" Fresh blood in Time's shrunk veins make mirth."

Harsh words they are, with gutturals and
sibilants crowding each other, and not to
be levelled and glossed into a satin surface.
Versifiers who make faultless lines to be
crooned in mystical tones will be disgusted.
And they have a right to a little sympathy,
— a very little. It is to be admitted
that the poems we have considered, "The
Cathedral," "The Footpath," and "Beaver
Brook," are not as easy reading as "We
are Seven;" furthermore, (that if Lowell,
had a nice sense of melody, it was subor-\
dinated to thought and energy) Not only
his genius was not lyrical,— in the sense of
excelling in *sing-able* verse, — but among
shorter poems there are few gems of predestined crystallization, and never any of
the verses written for sonorous effect, like

Coleridge's "In Xanada did Kubla Khan," etc. However, the poet in whose verse there is never anything to forgive seldom shows us anything to admire. If the soul of poetry is energy, its garment beauty, its effect emotion; if, according to Landor, "philosophy should run through poetry as veins do through the body;" if that is a poem which is inspired with original thought, graced by unborrowed pictures and figures, and which suggests continually more than meets the eye, then it will be impossible to ·deny Lowell a high rank among poets.

He is, indisputably, a poet, but, as already stated, more of a philosopher than a singer.[1]   And he is a poet of nature, with this addition, that when he sees a landscape he paints it, and, at the same time,

---

[1] As a notable example of the thought behind the thing,— just as the Egyptian priests, thousands of years ago, adored the Sun-God that was *behind* the sun,— the reader can look at Emerson's "Musketaquit." We have space only for a stanza : —

> "Thy summer voice, Musketaquit,
> Repeats the music of the rain:
> But sweeter rivers, pulsing, flit
> Through thee, than thou through Concord plain."

And the transcendental poet, B. W. Ball, in his poem to the Merrimack River, says, —

> "Thy sunny ripples, what are they
> If not reflections bright in me?"

looks *through* it, and perceives its true sig-
nificance and its ideal relations.   In this
way the mind is led from the visible image
to the thought behind it.

Poems with such a range, such vivid
conceptions, such high purpose, such keen
insight, such tender sympathy, and such
flashing lights of imagery, have never been
very common; and are not numerous enough
now, on either side of the Atlantic, to en-
danger Lowell's reputation.   After more
than forty years of beneficent influence,
attended by a constantly deepening interest, his poems may be left to take their •
chnace with posterity.

X.

A DISCIPLE of Lavater once said to the
writer, "There was never a great poet who
had not a long and generally a shapely
nose. Think of Wordsworth's profile, —
Tennyson's, Dante's. I know the nose on
Shakespeare's bust appears short, but I
distrust it; the pictures are better." The
writer thought to pose the physiognomist
by naming Keats; but he demurred, saying
that the position of the head in the common
engraving of Keats foreshortened the nose.

The writer then suggested that the rule
scarcely held in the case of Lowell. "That
is true," said he, "and it confirms my
theory. Lowell is a poet, but is not *all*
poet. If in one way he has great ideality,
comparison, and whatever other qualities
belong to a poet, he has also a marvellous
common-sense, like Ben Franklin, or Soc-
rates. His face shows this as clearly as
his writing and conversation. Never was
a man more solidly planted on the basis of
the understanding. When it comes to
reasoning he is acute, vigorous, aggressive:

no man has a surer or swifter parry or
thrust; only he tires of it at times, and,
giving way to his love of frolic, puts a *twist*
into a syllogism, which leaves his adversary
little to do but laugh."

It is not necessary to accept this reading
of Lowell's physiognomy; for, though many
men and all children are instinctive readers
of facial expression, it is probable there are
no exact and invariable correspondences between the forms of features and the qualities of mind.   But in respect to Lowell's
twofold mental character there is some
truth in the prognostication.   Even those
who knew him best were sometimes amazed
at the invincible logic in which his thought
took instant form; and there was never a
man quicker to hit the joint in the armor
of an adversary.   The solidity of his understanding, joined to his inborn skill in
statement and argument, was the foundation
of his power as a writer of prose.   In aid
of this native ability came the resources of
learning, and of wisdom, which is learning's mellow fruit; and his wide and varied
reading supplied him with illustrations
from every age and country.   His ideality
and plastic faculty gave to the train of
weighty thought the graces of image and

simile; and at length the sonorous sentences seemed moving to the sound of music, like a well-ordered army, glittering in sunlight.

Or, in another mood, the sentences became playful or ironic, and the listener or reader followed their course as one follows an electric car by its fitful sparkles.

It is not necessary to dwell upon the "Conversations on the Old Poets" (published in 1845), as he suffered that book to lapse. It contains many forcible and pungent passages, and shows originality and courage, but it lacks the mature richness, variety, and completeness of later works.

("Fireside Travels" is one of the most characteristic and charming of his volumes. Its leading Essay, "Cambridge Thirty Years Ago," contains reminiscences of the old town, the old times, and the old people, and especially of certain rare old college professors. No paper of Lowell's surpasses it in its youthful freshness, its quaint humor and picturesque memories. Other essays — "A Moosehead Journal," "In the Mediterranean," "Italy," etc. — are full of delightful touches, neither to be imitated nor described.

"In My Study Windows" there are glances without and within — studies of nature and of books. "My Garden Acquaintance" is a study of the birds, whose coverts were in the thick undergrowth that surrounded the grounds of Elmwood. "A Good Word for Winter" tells its own story. The paper on Lincoln was written before his tragic end, and before the united voices of our people had given him the place where he stands, among the greatest, if not the greatest, of American presidents. To read that article now is like reading prophecy, and its moral courage is refreshing and uplifting.

Probably the most brilliant of his lighter essays is that "On a Certain Condescension in Foreigners." The sentences gleam with wit, as from the play of polished swords. All forms of satire, irony, raillery, and sarcasm, are seen in it, but always in a quiet, bantering strain, and never with angry purpose. The delicate ridicule of the patronizing critics of our literature, institutions, and manners, is delicious. The airy grace of this sustained pleasantry is without parallel. Almost any other man capable of such a satire would have been sure to write it in a way to provoke a not unreasonable indignation on the part of those who were hit.

Another remarkable essay is "Democracy," in which epigrams seem to be the staple of the composition. With an easy flow like Montaigne's, there are occasional deep thoughts like Bacon's, and multitudes of felicitous turns that remind us of Swift and Sydney Smith. This is not to compare him to any of those great men; only to indicate certain obvious resemblances. But it would be difficult to find another essay combining such mature wisdom with such pungent and unexpected phrases, and animated with such inexhaustible spirit.

Among historical compositions, that entitled "New England Two Centuries Ago," and the address upon the Two Hundred and Fiftieth Anniversary of the Founding of Harvard College, are conspicuous. Under the poet's hand the life of the dead past is restored in its sombre beauty, its heroic devotion. The literary essays naturally are more numerous, and from them we gain a notion of the variety and extent of the reading on which they are founded.

The choice of subjects, if adequately treated, is often an indication of the power of an author. If Lowell had chosen to compete with the light and graceful writers, he might have given us specimens of admirable trifling; such as "Life at the Court of King René," "The Mystery of the Pentameron," "The Academia della Crusca," "Legends of the Rhine," and what not. But his innate good sense and the consciousness of power led him to choose the weightiest subjects, near to the hearts of mankind,— nothing less than a new survey of the chief landmarks of our literature. The list of authors treated includes Chaucer, Spenser, Shakespeare, Milton, Dryden, Fielding, Gray, Wordsworth, Coleridge, and Keats; and incidentally many others are referred to. He wrote also upon Dante, Lessing, and Rousseau; and if he had lived longer he would doubtless have given to the world his studies of Lope de Vega, Cervantes, and Goethe. So many critical estimates of the great English poets had been printed, one would think he would have found only dry straw to thresh; but in every instance he not only found something interesting to say, but either added to our knowledge or gave new points of view in regard to character and poetic art.[1]

---

[1] His essays upon the old English dramatists are appearing as this volume goes to press.

In estimating a character or a poem Lowell seldom used the destructive analytic method. He did not seek to affiliate a poet's philosophy,— as to Hegel or Spinoza, — nor to discover what proportion of this or that quality is found in his verse: metaphysical abstractions were not in his method. When one of the new critics has done with his "subject," it is not a *man* that the reader sees, but ticketed parcels and stoppered jars of primal elements, like the results of a chemical analysis. This method is often ingenious, and calls for admiration from those who do not know how a constructive critic works.

In reading Lowell's essay on Chaucer, that poet is re-created for us, touch by touch. We see him visibly rising in his proper person, with his native expression, and amid the surroundings of his time and place. It is like a sculptor's masterpiece, but in a finer element than clay; and as we look we may see the miracle of Pygmalion wrought anew. Even the creative soul is revealed to us in its own atmosphere.

Lowell had an intense sympathy with Chaucer. Both felt an abounding joy in nature; and Lowell could at least admire the master's genius in creating types of human character. For this and other valid reasons his essay is the most satisfactory, as it is the most brilliant, of any ever written upon that great poet. With great propriety it is dedicated to Professor Child, the poet's near friend, and one of the most eminent scholars in English.

In the article upon Shakespeare there is less absolute mastery, but it must be considered among the few memorable attempts to illustrate the poet's art, and to give him a solid footing among men. A complete view of the world of Shakespeare's creations would require a score of essays, but whoever knows this one well will have an impression as lasting as life.

In regard to the essay on Milton, friends of Professor Masson, his biographer and editor, thought some of Lowell's strictures rude and his phrases brutal. Lowell was combative, and in this instance perhaps discourteous. He was exasperated with the inordinate length and discursiveness of Masson's Life, and had no patience with his treatment of the subject; and the energy of Lowell's temperament got the better of his usually calm judgment. Some of the harsh phrases must be regretted; although those who remember the amenities that used to prevail among British reviewers will find that there have been plenty of precedents. At the same time, this essay will be long remembered for its general breadth of view, and for certain groups of majestic and sonorous sentences, — among the stateliest in modern English.

The article on Lessing is a model for a biographical sketch. It is full enough, but not burdened with dates or platitudes, and it contains an admirable view of German literature, and of Lessing's place in it. In the introduction there is some delightful banter upon the structure and crab-like movement of German sentences, and upon the mole-like predilections of certain German critics. There is nothing finer in the repertory of an "American humorist." On the whole, the essay is (to borrow a favorite collocation from our friends the booksellers) both "entertaining and instructive," and is the best account of a German *littérateur* obtainable in English.

The essay on Wordsworth was variously estimated in Great Britain. The special disciples of the poet, who, like their master, thought every line of his inspired, were shocked at the proposal to throw over about two-fifths as dull rubbish. But

Lowell celebrated the master's best verse in elaborate and picturesque sentences which are prose only in form; and whether readers agree or not to the "weeding out," all will admit that the praise of the remainder is worthy and noble. In the volume of Wordsworth's poems "chosen and edited by Matthew Arnold," it appears that Lowell's views are practically confirmed.

There is not space, even if it were desirable, to refer to all the essays; nor yet to the literary addresses which Lowell delivered on special occasions in Great Britain. In regard to the latter, every man who wields a pen, and who knows how much thought, judgment, scholarship, taste, and art go to the formation of clear, well-reasoned, allusive, and musical prose, recognizes the supremacy shown in them all. Exceptions may be taken to his judgments, but not to the literary art. Each specimen is like a piece of work from Benvenuto Cellini, perfect in design, perfect in the last detail.

It may be difficult to satisfy all minds in expressing an opinion upon Lowell's rank as a writer of prose. But there are minds so constituted as to become easily annoyed with sallies, however brilliant, when pursuing a serious subject. And there are those who object to allusions, mythologic, historic, or romantic, when they appear to be used, as some women use jewellery, to set off something that was well enough.before. And they will say that if a writer is to make a display of his powers, there can hardly be too much sparkle, within the limits of good taste, nor too many allusions, if apposite; but that if he feels a sense of duty in regard to his subject and his readers, he may hesitate about running down every metaphor which occurs to him, and bringing in recondite allusions which all but the very learned will have to leave unguessed. But there is no difficulty in recognizing Lowell's keen perception, the grasp of principles, the array of facts, precedents, and analogies, and the almost unparalleled power of witty and poetic illustration. Surely only a very unusual gravity would object to this.

We have before referred to the peculiar dualism of Lowell's mind: a strong current of reason running parallel with a creative imagination; and a serious purpose harmoniously co-existent with frolic, humor, and comic suggestion. We might think one of his inkstands filled by the spirit of

Fun, while the other was under the care of the sedatest of the Muses.

If we look at certain grave, sweet pages of Thackeray, Newman, Martineau, Matthew Arnold, and the Ruskin of thirty years ago, we feel that we have in them specimens of ideal English. Something of the calm dignity, the seemingly artless perfection, and the limpid movement, characteristic of those writers, may sometimes be seen in passages of Lowell; but his felicity in figures, and the irrepressible rush of his double stream of thought, often lead him into a style of writing that is both poetry and prose, and is not purely either. Hence his readers will be divided. With the reflective and philosophic an undue exuberance either of ornament or mirth is out of place. But there are others who read for the brilliancy of poetic illustration, and who believe that wisdom itself may be sportive without being taxed with folly; and to such the beauty and airy spirit of his sentences give an inexpressible delight.

As for the allusions, it may be said that all famous essays contain mineralogic finds, — from cairngorms to diamonds, — many of which will be beyond the appreciation of the unlearned. It is only a question of more or less. However this may be decided, it must be admitted that the combination of qualities in the essays makes them a storehouse of knowledge and a quarry for quotation; and endears them to men of ardent feeling and poetic insight, especially if they have had the advantages of general reading. Such men read with pure delight every sentence of Lowell, no matter upon what subject, — as they read every sentence of Thackeray.

In his own way Lowell is a master, and he will have the suffrages of admirers until some change comes to overturn the methods of our century; at the same time, with more simplicity and sobriety, or self-restraint, his circle of readers would have been limitless. In that case he would not have been Lowell.

XI.

In considering Lowell's character we are
struck by a bluff and determined honesty
which does not mince phrases for evil-
doers, nor make compromises with injus-
tice. His epigram upon the copyright
question, "The Ten Commandments Will
Not Budge," was everywhere quoted. But
certain poems upon plunderers and pecula-
tors in New York and elsewhere were conceived in such a spirit of wrath, and were
pervaded by such vitriolic phrases, that
they scorched whomsoever they touched.
The error was to take those special instances of official crime as characteristic of
a state or a period. Obviously it would
be unjust to stigmatize a whole people on
account of the robberies of a gang of poli-
ticians. The first rush of anger was natural, but when, years afterward, Lowell
was making a collection which should stand
with posterity as part of his mature convictions, he struck out " The World's Fair, "
and probably other poems which were the

expressions of a temporary mood.   Though
the spirit which prompted them was noble
and courageous, it would seem that he was
right in cancelling them; they had served
a temporary purpose, but they did not belong with his well-reasoned and maturely
considered poems.

Although these poems are omitted from
Lowell's ''complete works,'' and in defer-
ence to his wishes are not reproduced in
this volume, it may be that when a generation has passed, and the history of this century is written, they may need less apology,
and may even constitute a claim to the admiration of posterity.   For it is evident
that we are groping now in an eclipse of justice.   There is no check upon great crim-
inals, no punishment for colossal crime.
For theft to be honorable it needs only to
be done on a grand scale; the larceny of a
jackknife leads to the house of correction,
but stealing a railroad and ruining thousands of bond-and-stockholders is good
financiering.   Millionnaires, gorged with
plunder, attend church.   One might reasonably ask if, with pliant clergymen, the
Ten Commandments do *not* budge?   Have
the wreckers of railroad companies in New
York, or of insurance companies in Hart-

ford, ever been hit from the pulpits of the churches where they "worship"?

We may ask in simple phrase what has become of the Ten Commandments and the Golden Rule, in business, politics, or in society at large? What is the religion or morality of the numberless combinations to put up prices? What law or what sentiment of justice restrains the capitalists who are turning this country into an enclosed hunting-field wherein their fellow-men are the game?

It was the growing pressure of this evil spirit which moved the soul of Lowell, and which will stir the souls of others in larger and larger circles, until there is a return to old-fashioned honesty, or a plunge into chaos.

The subject of Lowell's religious opinions is not likely to be definitely settled. In his young manhood he used to mention with evident satisfaction that his father had never called himself a Unitarian; that he was simply pastor of a Congregational Church, and a friend of Channing,—nothing more. In the course of an acquaintance of thirty years the present writer never heard him utter a word upon the doctrine of the Trinity; it was only inferred from various circumstances that he sympathized with his father's views.   In his poems it is seen how little stress he laid upon creed; they only inculcate brotherhood, piety, and love.   There was never an irreligious tone in his conversation, but he seldom went to church until he reached middle age; and when he went it was generally with his wife to the Episcopal service.

He was pained and almost angry at the lengths to which the more "advanced" liberals were going.   He was vehemently opposed to modern materialistic doctrines; [1] and, as heretofore related, declared that for his part he would not "believe that Hamlet sprang from a clod."   He loved the Bible, often referred to the Book of Job, loved the beauty of a ritual, loved things established; and meanwhile his belief did not appear to be really fixed upon any system.   It is a long step from the simple ethics of the Sermon on the Mount to a metaphysical creed.

The sense of justice which made him a reformer was an ever-present ideal, but appeared to have been evolved from the

[1] A glimpse of his thought and feeling is shown in *Credidimus Jovem Regnare.*

intellectual side; while, by instinct and habit, he was (sentimentally) a conservative in every fibre of his being. The reader will see a fine specimen of an almost paradoxical analysis in the opening portion of "Fitz Adam's Story." With a less clear intellect, and a less faithful conscience, he might have remained on the other side. For among reformers there were some who outran his convictions and were antipathetic in various ways. The name "crank," had not then been invented. Some wished to destroy the church, because it had been "the bulwark of American Slavery." Lowell did not wish to destroy an institution which had power for good, but rather to see it built up; and, besides, a church with a long history behind it was to him beautiful and venerable for its own sake. He said more than once that if the Calvinistic churches were to be judged by the results of their teachings upon character and conduct, as seen in Scotland and New England, those churches were entitled to the highest place. For, he said, the superiority was not solely in morality and intelligence, but in the prevalent sense of duty, in high ideals and inflexible principles, and, in short, in the consciousness of the spirit-

ual world that was an eternal NOW with be-
lievers. After due allowance made for
hypocrites and time-servers, he thought
there were among Calvinists more godly
men, each living —

" As ever in his great Taskmaster's eye,"

than in any other branch of the Christian
church. And one day he added, to the
writer's infinite surprise, that, considered
as a set of intellectual propositions, the
"five points" appeared to form a theory
about as reasonable as any other. He
seemed to advance this tentatively, as he
might have put forth a metaphysical spec-
ulation, and not to intimate that he had a
fixed belief in it. This was some fifteen
years ago, and the thought may have been
temporary. The Rev. Dr. Savage lately in
a public discourse said that, in the course
of a conversation two or three years ago,
Lowell told him he presumed his general
views upon religion were in the main those
which he (Dr. Savage) held. This was
for Lowell an unusual confidence. Possibly the contending theories were from
time to time alternately in light and in
shadow. But the doctrines of his poems,

reverence, love, and brotherhood, never suffered eclipse or change.

It would be difficult to mention his favorite authors, for as time went by he was continually laboring in new fields. Among his early treasures were Froissart, — in a manner the Walter Scott of his age, — and Marco Polo, Purchas, and Hakluyt, authors who carried with them a largeness akin to nobility, and who, if they did not write poems, often suggested poetry. Milton's line, —

" And airy tongues that syllable men's names,"

Lowell said, was from Marco Polo. Of the old dramatists he was most fond of Marlowe; as for Chapman, he preferred his Homer to his plays. He admired the well-ordered sentences and beautful images of Jeremy Taylor; the style of Hooker, earliest of great prose-writers, and of Latimer and South. Undoubtedly he had read the works of Lord Bacon, but he never spoke of him. He had an unspeakable aversion to maxims like Rochefoucauld's, which include a kernel of selfishness or an innuendo of baseness.

He *lived* in the intellectual light of

Shakespeare. He often read passages of Chaucer to friends, and loved to point out the master-strokes which described a person and revealed his character. It may be stated here, somewhat out of place, that Lowell once hoped to write a New England poem after the manner of the "Canterbury Tales," sketching a group of people at a nooning in the field, but after "Fitz Adam's Story" he went no farther. The reason is not far to seek. The burdens he assumed in the university, his constant and severe studies, and his subsequent duties as minister, combined to lead him away from the fresh, joyous, creative mood in which such a composite and many-colored poem could have been fashioned.

This reference to favorite books is necessarily brief. The attentive reader of his essays, of "The Fable for Critics," and of special poems, like that in memory of Agassiz, and those upon Longfellow, Holmes, Quincy and Wyman will learn more than can be told here. But it may be said he talked often about Emerson, and with special admiration about Hawthorne. He said to the writer he would not venture a comparison between the latter and Shakespeare, but he believed the world would sooner see

another Shakespeare than another Hawthorne.

Among English contemporaries he admired Tennyson and Arthur Hugh Clough, ₁
made only brief and respectful references to
Browning, and loved Thackeray. Back in
the fifties Clough was for a year Lowell's
near neighbor in Cambridge.

It is singular that Thackeray had an im-
perfect appreciation of Lowell's poetry.
He said to the author of this volume (July,
1857), "With such a genius for comedy,—
greater, I believe, than any English poet
ever had, — with such wit, drollery, Yankee
sense and spirit, I wonder he does not see
his 'best hold,' and stick to it. Why a
man who can delight the world with such
creations as *Hosea Biglow* should insist
upon writing second-rate serious verse I
cannot see." And there was much more of
the same sort. He evidently loved Lowell,
for, in speaking of him a little later, a spray
of tears bedimmed his large spectacles; but
he could not see any merit or "extenuating
circumstances" in his serious verse.

It was not for a young man of thirty to
argue with the leading writer of Great
Britain, but he stated his opinion modestly,
and then changed the subject. For obvious

reasons this conversation was never fully reported during Lowell's lifetime.

Do we yield to Thackeray's judgment, given so long ago? By no means. Experience has shown that authors are not infallible, unless in special lines, and that men without creative genius often have wider sympathies and sounder judgment. Emerson's "Parnassus" is profoundly interesting as showing the direction of his reading, his opinions, and tastes, but as a collection of English poetry it is one of the most incomplete and unsatisfactory ever made. Thackeray was a great man, and a greater artist, in a certain sphere, but he had never any perception or consciousness of an ideal world. His conception of poetry may, perhaps, be not unfairly gauged by his gay and vivacious ballads. It is true, Lowell had not then written "The Cathedral" or "The Commemoration Ode."

Complaints were made during Lowell's last years of his forbidding manners; and there were intimations that he was less American at heart than British; but nothing is more certain than the persistence of his patriotic feeling and his courage to express it under all circumstances. A notable instance occurred at the dinner of the Society of Authors in London at which Lowell made one of his perfect speeches. He told the audience, in substance, that Great Britain had been in the wrong in both of the contests with the United States; and that the last war (1812) though insignificant, and not creditable to either party, in a military point of view, was just and necessary; and that by the abatement of Great Britain's pretensions to the sovereignty of the seas, and to the right of search, international law had been advanced, and the whole world was the gainer. These were not his words, but what he said was said most impressively; and every hearer felt that there was a calm courage behind the utterance. Furthermore, he was always firm in regard to what he considered the justice due to Ireland, though of course he could take no part, while minister, in a British domestic question.

As to manners, a man of seventy who has passed through vicissitudes is seldom effusive, and Lowell certainly was no exception to the rule. People who expected that Hosea Biglow would be found sitting on a gate in Hyde Park, whittling and telling stories, were hardly prepared to see a rather stately man in faultless dress, whose steady eyes repelled familiarity, and sometimes rebuked pretension.

The origin of the ill-feeling towards Lowell was in the false idea that still prevails among our people as to the duties of a minister at London. The rich and fashionable who visit that capital think his chief duty is to present them at court; and that the ceremony is an affair about which there should be no more difficulty than in visiting the Tower or the Zoölogical Garden. There are other supposed duties, such as writing letters of introduction for ambitious people to a great poet, novelist, or other celebrity; also looking up in the Herald's College, or in remote parochial registers, genealogies, and evidence of descent from shadowy ancestors; also recovering fortunes, — always on deposit at the Bank of England, and crying out for their lawful owners — besides occasionally cashing or guaranteeing doubtful checks. The evil has become oppressive for ministers, and even for consuls, who could many a tale unfold.

Now the British Government, with great courtesy, allows the American minister to

present a reasonable number of his country
men and women. But any one who knows
how great is the crush of British people
who have the best right to attend these
functions, — the *necessary* presentation of
civil and military officers, young and old,
upon being commissioned or promoted;
the presentation of the daughters of peers
and gentlemen who *must* appear at court,
and of the diplomatic body, including sec-
retaries and *attachés;* — any one who knows
the facts will see that the presence of foreigners is a grace which is not to be abused.
Very few can be presented without infrin-
ging indubitable rights in which our people
have no share. No such crowds are ever
pushing to the English court from France,
Germany, or other European country; but
Americans, though often politically hostile,
and sometimes discourteous, to British
officials, seem to think they have only to
ask, and the gates of St. James should fly
open. Every American minister for the
last thirty years has had his patience
completely exhausted by the persistent desire of his country-women to wear their
trains and diamonds in the presence of
the Queen. The pressure was calmly and
steadfastly resisted by Lowell, and with

the natural result. It is almost certain
that many of the reports of Lowell's aris-
tocratic and chilling manners came from
disappointed aspirants.

Few Americans of real distinction have
desired to be "presented."   Many have
lived in Great Britain for years without
once thinking of it.   A man may respect
the Queen as a sovereign and as a woman,
and yet not desire to embarrass his minister or the lord chamberlain, nor to put on
an obsolete and uncomfortable suit for the
sake of passing with a bow before her
majesty.

As has been more than once said, Lowell
wrote with extreme care, but none of his
prose appeared in book form until after it
had been kept, considered, and carefully
gone over.   He was inaccessible to offers
of money for articles or poems; and in the
last years of his life enormous sums were
named as ready for any contributions from
his pen.   But he wrote only when a subject
came to him naturally, and when to write
was a pleasure and a duty.   Had he been
avaricious, or even reasonably "thrifty,"
he could have earned a large income.   As
it was, he earned enough for his wants,
and wrote enough for his fame.   Some of

the possessors of great incomes from literature find in the end that their wealth is
their chief reward; Fame being chary of
laurels, and seldom bestowing them on
those who abuse her patience.

Lowell left a small estate, but a good
name, which is better than riches. His
love for his *alma mater* was shown by his
bequest of such books in his collection as
the college library did not possess. He
watched the growth of Harvard with the
deepest interest and pride.

His association with public life, though
flattering and honorable, was only an incident in his career; it was as a scholar, in-
structor, essayist, and poet that he realized
his early aspirations and fulfilled his
destiny.

He left his letters and MSS. in the care
of his friend Norton, the faithful and ac-
complished editor of Carlyle's correspondence. His letters must be full of interest, as a record of his life, as containing
the seed-thoughts of his works, and as
showing the play of his delightful humor.

His career furnishes an impressive lesson for American youths. He made the
most of his talents and opportunities. He
loved books, studies, the beauty of the

outer world, his art, and his fellow men; but chiefly he kept his eyes fixed on lofty ideals, and always listened to the voice of conscience.   He measured duty by absolute standards, and compromised nothing of principle.   With such a character, even without his phenomenal gifts and graces, he would have been A Great Man.

A BIBLIOGRAPHY:

FOR THE ASSISTANCE OF READERS AND STUDENTS.

In the list following it is believed that each work is mentioned, with the date of its original publication. But there is no attempt to give all the various new editions, new combinations or arrangements of works which the publishers have placed before the public.

CLASS POEM [1] 1838

A YEAR'S LIFE AND OTHER POEMS . . 1841

THE PIONEER. A Magazine. Nos. I.,
  II., and III. 1843

---

[1] In the narration preceding it will be seen that Lowell was "in exile" at the time when the "Class Poem" was to be read. It is dated at "Concord, August, 1838." In the Preface the author says, "Many of my readers and all of my friends know that it was not by any desire of mine that this rather slim production is printed. Circumstances known to all my readers, and which I need not dilate on here, *considerably cooled my interest in the performance.*" The poem covers 45 pages of close type, and, considering the age of the writer (19), is a piece of strong and free versification. In its substance it is mainly a satire upon the abolitionists, and upon the progressives in religion and politics. The suggestion is that the Indian is more deserving of sympathy than the African. The use of the phrase "clothes-philosophy" shows that Lowell had already read "Sartor Resartus."

ADDRESS AT THE DEDICATION OF THE
LIBRARY IN CHELSEA, MASS   .   .   .   1885

DEMOCRACY, AND OTHER ADDRESSES .   1886

[Containing: Democracy; Dean Stanley; Fielding; Coleridge; Books and Libraries; Wordsworth; Don Quixote; and Harvard's 250th Anniversary.]

POLITICAL ESSAYS   1888

[Containing: The American Tract Society; The
Election in November; E Pluribus Unum;
The Pickens-and-Stealins Rebellion; General
McClellan's Report; The Rebellion, Its
Causes and Consequences; McClellan or Lin-
coln? Reconstruction; Scotch the Snake or
kill It? The President on the Stump; The
Seward-Johnson Reaction; The Place of the
Independent in Politics.]

HEARTSEASE AND RUE   1888

THE INDEPENDENT IN POLITICS. Address before the N.Y. Reform Club   .   1888

A FABLE FOR CRITICS. With portraits
of authors .   .   .   .   ,   .   .   .   1890

LITERARY AND POLITICAL ADDRESSES .   1891

[Contents the same as in "Democracy," with
three additions; viz., Tariff Reform, The Independent in Politics, and Our Literature.]

COMPLETE WORKS IN TEN VOLUMES .   1891

LATEST LITERARY ESSAYS AND AD-
DRESSES. Edited by Professor Norton.   1891

[Containing: Gray; Landor; Walton; Milton's
Areopagitica; Richard III.; Modern Languages; Progress of the World.]

THE OLD ENGLISH DRAMATISTS. Edited by Professor Norton 1892

[Containing : Marlowe, Webster, Chapman, Beaumont and Fletcher, Massinger and Ford; with an Introduction.]

The Twelve Lectures on English Poets and Poetry delivered in 1854-55 were fully reported in the *Boston Daily Advertiser*, but have not been collected.

AFTER–THOUGHTS

THE first after-thought of an author becomes a preface, and serves as an inclined plane to get the reader up to the subject. Later, when the pages are stereotyped, other belated thoughts may arise, chiefly regrets for omissions, and for the want of qualifications of general statements ; and these may be an inclined plane to let the reader down.

After-thoughts are inevitable when, as in the present instance, an unusual brevity has been aimed at. With greater fulness a more truthful impression would be given to those who only partially know the circumstances.

It should be borne in mind that though this is intended to be a reasonably complete view of Lowell's life (in miniature), yet the intimate, personal part of the narrative belongs mainly to the period between 1853 and 1859. After 1860 the circle of his friends expanded, and was intersected by other and larger circles, until — after the overthrow of slavery — it would have been difficult to find a literary or a fashionable

135

man in Boston who would admit that he had not *always* admired Lowell, and *always* opposed slavery.

In regard to Lowell's early friends, mention has been made chiefly of neighbors; there were many in Boston and elsewhere to whom he was warmly attached. One of these was Charles W. Storey, a vivacious, witty, and delightful man, whom Lowell always called his solicitor. Another was Edmund Quincy, a man of rare ability and courtly manners, — a picked man of countries. As he and Lowell had been co-workers in the anti-slavery cause they were united by close ties. The rare gatherings of Quincy's friends at Bankside were memorable.

—— It may be mentioned that Lowell would not, or could not, look upon the face of a dead friend. The writer went with him to Quincy's funeral, and he declined to enter the room where the coffin was. He said he *could* not; that his repugnance, dread, or *malaise*, was not to be overcome.

A further qualification must be made more prominent, in regard to literary friends. There was never a time in which his relations with Professor Child, George William Curtis, the Nortons of Shady Hill, and some others, were not intimate, tender, and trustful. So with his numerous relatives in the region. This is to be taken *in connection* with the gatherings on Sunday afternoons, and the Friday whist club.

—— Who was Robert Carter, so frequently mentioned?

We shall all have to be "explained" some day. He was a man of enormous reading, Prescott's secretary; afterward an able political journalist; and finally *advocatus diaboli*, or final corrector, in the office of Appleton's Cyclopædia. He lived first near "The Willows," afterwards in Sparks Street, then an unknown region.

> "For Sparks Street is a dark street,
> And succory grows in Sparks Street, —
> And lamp-posts *everywhere!* "

So ran the ballad, doubtless Lowell's. Carter was short, plump, and very near-sighted; full of spirits, though quiet in manner, and with a memory that was never at fault. Lowell, who had names for most of his friends, called him "Don Roberto," or "The Don."

Notice in the rhymed preface to the "Fable for Critics: —

"I can walk with the Doctor, get facts from the Don, or draw out the Lambish quintessence of John." The "Doctor" was his brother-in-law, Howe; and "John," of course, was John Holmes, whose unfailing humor was much like that of Charles Lamb.

Carter's only book was "A Summer Cruise on the Coast of New England." It ran through many editions. Mrs. Carter wrote some delightful children's books, among them " The Great Rosy Diamond," which after forty years still retains its popularity.

The little house in Sparks Street long ago gave place to modern villas, but it remains in memory as one of the alternate stations of the whist club.

—— John Bartlett says that Lowell, some months before his death, sat down with him, John Holmes, and Charles F. Choate, and they all strove to bring back the light and warmth of long ago. In the old times Lowell always proposed the toast of " THE CLUB " with great emphasis ; and on this occasion,— the last on earth, as it proved to be, — he gave the old toast with evident emotion, as shown by a break in his voice and a quivering of the eyelids. It was about that time when the striking but rather pathetic photograph of Lowell was taken by Pach.